BARBARA J. LANGNER

The Detectives Who Loved Shakespeare

ISBN: 0-6157-0220-1
ISBN-13: 9780615702209

I

"A power hungry ruler imprisons a beautiful woman in a cave to die of starvation. What a story!" Monica rubbed the back of her neck while talking to her fellow teacher of English Lit. during the passing break at Four Hills High School. "The students always want to know the reason, and I tell them curiosity is the backbone of education."

"*Antigone* is a great play. I love teaching it, but when I bring out the book and the kids see the name of the author, they start to yawn," said Leslie as she watched a student open his locker and throw his books inside. Folded pieces of paper dribbled out of a history book and added to the locker debris of gum wrappers, coke cans, and wads of balled up paper.

"Sophocles sounds stuffy. I try to jazz up my introduction by telling them we have rulers today who also kill their citizens for disobeying unjust laws, but they still sneak their phones out of their pockets and text under their desks." Monica pushed up the sleeve of her sweater in order to check her watch.

"I have an idea. Let's invite John Spenser, the prominent peace activist, to speak to our classes. He's going to be here in Albuquerque this weekend at a big peace conference. He always mentions civil disobedience as an alternative to injustice, especially when a country drafts young men for a war."

Monica thought about the suggestion for a minute. "Maybe he would come. The kids would like to hear an adult who favors rebellion, especially if his name would annoy their middle class parents. Sure, let's go to the conference and ask him."

The next day the two young teachers wandered around the lobby of the Barclay Towers Hotel as they waited for John Spenser's lecture. The vendors had spread out their wares on tables that stretched over the entire lobby. They stopped at a display of Guatemalan insect energy bars.

"I'm going to run a marathon in two weeks. I could use some energy bars," said Leslie as she inspected the different types of chopped insects: grasshopper, tick, and ant.

She looked up at the vendor and asked, "Are these insect bars made of vegetables? I'm a vegetarian."

"Yes, Ma'am, these bars are 100% vegetable, just like eating corn or beans. They'll give you lots of energy, especially the tick bar. That's my favorite."

Monica whispered, "He's pulling your leg. Those bars aren't vegetable, and besides I don't think it's healthy to eat bugs."

Leslie, however, pulled out her money and bought one of each variety. "You have a closed mind. People have eaten insects for thousands of years."

Monica shrugged her shoulders and continued walking to the next table.

Both young women in their twenties taught English 12. Although they were both Democrats and environmentalists, they dressed in different styles. Monica wore a stylish, red sweater set with her jeans while Leslie's long, linen dress and several necklaces of red, yellow, and blue beads gave her a hippie look from an earlier time.

One table exhibited an exotic array of turtle shells hand painted by pygmies from Zaire. Another displayed cups made of dried gourds from Tanzania. Leslie headed for the yellow and green gourd cups. "What do you think of these? Wouldn't they go great on my seaweed mats?" She picked one up and peered into the bowl part. When she set it down, it wobbled.

"You can't put them in the dishwasher, and those seaweed mats of yours are crumbling away. Buy a tee shirt instead."

"You're right. Let's sit down for a moment. I have a pebble in my shoe." Leslie fished out a tiny rock from her Birkenstock shoe.

"While we're here, I thought I might get an idea for a novel I'm writing. I'd like to write a murder mystery like the old Agatha Christe books where ten people spend a weekend in an old country estate. I could use a hotel or bed and breakfast."

"I hope you get some ideas, but remember we're here to get John Spenser to talk to our classes about injustice and the law."

"Sure, I'm all for it." Monica stood up. "Since we still have a little time before his speech, let's look at some more of the weird stuff." They wandered over to a table where a vendor sold edible jewelry made of dried cranberries, walnuts, and raisins.

The vendor made his pitch. "These necklaces are what we call in the business 'one timers.' You wear the necklace, come home, and eat it. If you prefer, you can snack on it while you wait in the doctor's office, a bank, or just anyplace. It's a fun food."

The two women said in unison, "Thanks. We're just looking."

On the next table, another vendor displayed brightly colored macaroni necklaces. The sign said, "Necklaces Made by Midgets in Wyoming."

Aroused by curiosity, Monica asked the seller, "Is there a colony of midgets in Wyoming? I've never heard of any. Occasionally a circus has advertised a midget in a freak show, but I've never heard of a group of them." As she spoke, she examined a pink necklace to determine if the midgets used crayons or felt pens to color the macaroni.

"Well, Ma'am, I shouldn't tell you this, but those midgets are Girl Scouts." He lowered his voice to a whisper. "My boss is trying to help out his daughter's troupe, so he sells them at conventions. When we go to conferences like this one, we gear our advertising to the participants, if you know what I mean."

"Did you get the idea from the pygmy shell painters?" asked Monica.

"As a matter of fact, we did. I talked to the vendor, and he told me he's sold a lot of turtle shells. I don't know what people do with them, but they sell." He scratched his chin and pointed to a table next to him. "That guy sells yak butter chocolates in a tin box decorated by indentations made in the metal by human teeth. He says the Tibetans do the decorating of the tin, but really he uses a pair of false teeth to make the marks. He sells them as hostess gifts, and he's doing a good business."

Monica turned toward Leslie. "I'm going to buy the yak butter chocolates since I could always use a hostess gift. See, I'm very open minded." Monica walked over to the table that had stacks of tin boxes with different designs. Eight chocolates were tucked into each box.

After selecting one, she handed it to the Hispanic, not Tibetan, salesman who wrapped the tin box up. He pointed to the lid which had indentations in the form of a flower. "Those were made by my fellow Tibetans trained in the art of tooth decoration. You'll not find any gift like this anywhere in the world except here, or in Tibet, of course."

Monica didn't mention his fellow vendor had ratted on him. She just paid for her purchase and walked on.

Piles of tee shirts with various pictures of doves in flight or at rest lay on the next table. Leslie bustled over to check out the designs. "I don't care if I have a lot of tee shirts. I've got to get one of these."

"I'll wander around while you shop." Since none of the wares interested her, Monica sidled over to the closed ballroom doors and cracked one open. As she peeped in the crevice, she saw a man in jeans and a black tee shirt stride down the center aisle, leap over the bottom step to the stage, stumble, and regain his balance before prancing to the microphone.

"John, if you're going to do that leap, you have to do it right. If you stumble, you'll appear old. You've got to look young and vibrant," instructed an attractive woman dressed in a gauzy, long garment with blue and yellow beads.

"Don't worry, Randy. I can do it. I just lost my footing." He pulled out a pocket mirror, smoothed his blond hair back, and inspected the skin around his eyes. "I look young. I can pass for 32 or 33."

"Yes, you look young. No one would ever guess you're 52."

Monica couldn't tell from her tone of voice if she was being sarcastic or not.

"Don't ever say my age. Someone could be listening." He shifted his eyes back and forth over the empty room. "By the way, I want to sell my own brand of tee shirt. I have a great design in mind that should appeal to the Star Wars crowd. In the center will be a picture of me with a sword and the words 'John Spenser Fights for Peace.'"

"I didn't know you liked irony. I'll tell Jeff to look into all the details, but right now we need to check out everything for your speech. Do you have your notes?"

"I don't need notes. It's all up here," boasted John as he pointed to his head.

Monica slowly closed the door and sought out her friend who had a plastic bag on her arm. "I heard a very interesting conversation. I'll tell you when no one can overhear us."

After doing some more looking and pricing, Monica noticed the crowd was thinning. "It must be time for the lecture. Let's head for the ballroom." Always efficient, Monica clutched a legal pad and pen for note taking while Leslie carried a huge tote embroidered with pink and red flowers. Monica realized Leslie blended in with the swarm of women in colorful folk dresses, sandals and freshly washed faces devoid of makeup while she in her twin sweater set and lipstick looked a little too middle class for the peace crowd.

As they entered the ballroom, Monica saw a man in a three-piece suit tapping the mike, adjusting the volume of the speakers, and moving cords around. He put a bottle of water on the shelf inside the podium. While they looked for seats, the man in the suit walked to the back of the ballroom where Monica could see a light board, boxes, and circles of cord.

Monica and Leslie didn't find any available seats until they got to the back. They had to sit in the last row, directly in front of the equipment area. Sounds of scuffing, murmurs, and coughing filled the air, but Monica could still hear the man in jeans and black tee shirt hiss, "What's the name of the African country that's in the middle of a war? I need the name, rather than just a continent. It's more effective."

Monica couldn't understand the muffled reply, but a second later the same voice yelped, "God damn it. That's what I pay you for." After another minute, the voice said, "Did you put the vodka in the water bottle? You know I need a good belt to keep me going."

Monica didn't hear any more complaints so she assumed he had received an affirmative reply. She took a quick peek and concluded The Suit was the employee of John Spenser whose words certainly didn't fit the image of a compassionate, loving, seeker of peace.

In a few minutes, John strode down the middle of the aisle, took the stairs to the stage two at a time without stumbling, and made the peace sign with his fingers. While clapping, whooping and chanting, "Peace, peace, peace," the members of the audience all stood. The crowd added foot pounding, which amplified the noise considerably.

This excitement continued for about five minutes until John made a little bowing gesture with his hands pressed together prayerfully. The welcoming hubbub ended. Monica felt he had perfect timing. If he had allowed the ovation to continue too long, he would have appeared to be a little vain, but now he appeared humble. Everyone settled down and waited to hear from the master.

He started with the demented motives dictators used to initiate violence. He gave examples of wholesale carnage and specific cases of gruesome deaths. After a particularly horrific story of a little girl who received a blast from a flame thrower, John sniffed and wiped an eye with his finger.

People in the audience dug in their purses and pockets for tissues to dry their tears. John made sort of a throat clearing sound as if he were trying to get hold of himself. He reached for his bottle of water, unscrewed the top and took a swig. John appeared to be summoning his will to continue even though he was overcome with grief. He swallowed another slug, set the bottle down, and continued with his lecture.

During his speech, John's voice rose high and fell; he speeded up and slowed down for emphasis. He repeated the phrase, "We want peace now." The audience members chanted with him and stomped their feet for emphasis. His speech electrified the participants. Because of their enthusiastic response, Monica concluded the audience saw him as a revered guru while she saw him as a skilled performer. He continued to talk about the horrors of war and the necessity for everyone to become part of the peace movement.

After a particularly grim example of a teenage boy who had burned to death while trying to rescue his mother during a bomb attack, he begged the crowd to contribute to a fund called "Peace for Africa." As the ushers passed baskets up and down the aisles, he said, "Cash was preferable, but checks were welcome too." As a closing gesture, John made a deep bow while putting his hands into a prayer position. The crowd again stood and clapped for this vibrant, but modest man, who spent his life working to improve the world.

Leslie pulled out four twenties from her purse, while Monica frowned at this large amount of money. "Are you sure you want to give that much to his cause?"

"Of course," replied Leslie, "he's wonderful, and he's helping mankind."

Monica thought about John's words she had overheard before the speech which pointed out his vanity. Could a true lover of peace be concerned about personal appearance? She embraced his cause but doubted his sincerity. Because of her mixed feelings, she only threw a meager five into the basket as it came down the row.

After the ushers had finished gathering the contributions, John walked down the steps and waded through the crowd spilling into the aisles.

"Let's ask him to speak to our classes," Leslie said in an excited voice. "I know his talk doesn't really fit in with *Antigone*, but maybe he could sort of bring in the subject of civil disobedience and the war in Viet Nåm. I'm sure if we asked him, he would talk about the lives lost in that war."

"He might not want to talk to school classes since they won't be contributing to his cause, but we have nothing to lose. Yes, let's ask him."

They had to wait awhile. At first a large group surrounded him but later thinned out to just a few star-struck disciples.

Leslie joined the smaller circle and gushed, "You were wonderful. I'd love to have my students exposed to your captivating and important message. Would you be able to speak to a couple high school classes that are studying *Antigone*?"

John smiled beatifically at her and the group. "I would love to, my dear, but I have many obligations. I'll speak to my assistant and have her check my calendar. I'll tell her to give you a call."

Monica quickly pulled out her legal pad, wrote down their phone numbers on a piece of paper, and was about to hand it to him when an attractive woman in a long, gauzy dress approached the little group. Monica recognized her as the lady who had given instructions to John about leaping on the stage when she had peeked through the opening in the door.

The woman sidled over to John, touched his arm in a proprietary way, and murmured, "Let's go, darling."

John bent down and spoke to her in a low voice. "Just a minute, Randy, we need to check with Jeff about a couple of things first." Monica and Leslie politely backed away so he could have more privacy, but then abruptly he and Randy strode off while he gave a final wave to his inner circle.

"He doesn't have our phone numbers. How can he contact us?" asked Leslie as she watched the retreating figures.

"Let's follow him. I'll hand over the paper, thank him, and dash off. I don't think that would be too offensive," said Monica while she put her Bic pen back in her purse.

Both of them followed the pair to a small room off the ballroom. When John and Randy entered the room, they pushed the door shut, but it didn't quite close. Monica could see through the sliver of light the back of the man wearing the navy blue suit. He was counting money and stacking it in neat piles on the desk. She moved closer to the door and put her hand up to knock but hesitated and listened instead.

"How much did we take in, Jeff?" asked John as he leaned over the table and spoke to The Suit.

"The checks amounted to $2200 and the cash is about $600 although I still have a few small bills left."

Jeff wet his thumb with his tongue and continued counting bills.

John scooped up the cash and stuffed it in his pocket. "That's close enough for me. Let's head out for dinner and order a good wine. We deserve a little relaxation. We can put the checks and the rest of the money in the bank account tomorrow after I collect more from my last speech. We'll use the money for a nice vacation in Florida. Too bad the convention doesn't run for a week. We could get a little more."

"What's going to happen when the convention officials find out you had a special collection. According to the rules, the attendees pay for the convention in one payment only, and that's it," said Jeff as he stood up and put the checks in a zippered money bag

"Don't worry. I'll get my fee from them tomorrow after my speech, and they'll never know. Besides I can always play the innocent I-didn't-know role. By the way, you need to put more vodka in my water bottles. I need a stiff drink when I'm out there giving my spiel."

Randy had been silent through this conversation, but she finally threw out a suggestion for tomorrow's special collection. "Urge them to throw in cash instead of checks. Besides all the bother about putting the checks in and taking the money out, there still is a record of the transactions at the bank. I worry about that a little."

"Don't worry about the bank. No one will ever notice anything out of the ordinary."

Randy removed her tangled strands of beads and chucked them in her purse. "I'm tired of wearing this junk. I don't think this flower child image helps at all."

"You two act like whining babies. We have to dress like money is unimportant to us. The cause is all we care about. Jeff, you can wear a suit if you want because you aren't part of the show, but you, Randy, are quite visible since you organize the offertory. Also, you help me out with the college kids who always get enthused after my speech and want to start a campus club." John finished his tirade and glared at his employees

After hearing this admission of fraud, Leslie and Monica stared at each other with open mouths in shock. Leslie grabbed Monica's arm in her frustration. "I believed him! He just snatched up all that money, including my 80 bucks, and put it in his pocket. I want my money back. And it's not just me, but he duped all those people. Isn't there something we can do?"

Monica made a shushing sound. "He'll hear you. I'd like to see him rot in jail, but I don't know if we have the power to do anything. He'll deny saying what we just heard." After a pause, she added, "If he talks to our students, do you think he'll pass a basket and try to get their lunch money?"

While the two were whispering, the door suddenly opened. John stiffened when he saw the two young women just inches from the door. After a brief silence, he cleared his throat and said, "Could I help you?"

Monica desperately tried to think of some reason they were there by the door. "Ah, I, or rather we, want to give you our phone numbers, for the presentation to our classes, but you're probably busy. We *just* got here a second ago, and here's the paper, but I know you're busy with the convention and all but we *just* got here a second ago," stammered Monica who realized she had spoken a run-on sentence.

Silence. John extended his hand and took the paper. "I'll let you know if I have the time."

"Ah, thank you," mumbled Monica, and the two walked backward a few steps before turning around and making their exit.

"Do you think he knows we heard all that stuff? And what would he do if he did know?" Leslie clutched her big flowered tote and whispered to Monica while they charged down the hall to the lobby.

"I don't think he'll 'off us' if that's what you're implying." Monica hoped she used the correct gangster lingo. "We'll never see him again. He doesn't want to speak to our classes. That's obvious." Monica kept her voice low as they walked since many of the convention participants were milling about like ants.

"But remember, he has to do something with the bank account before he leaves town. Maybe we should warn the bank. Maybe we should inform the convention officials. Maybe we should tell someone," sputtered Leslie.

"Yes, you're right. We should do something." Monica's conscience was kicking in. "Who was that philosopher who said if you saw a crime and didn't try to stop it, you, too, were guilty?"

"I don't know his name, but I agree. Let's tell someone."

Monica got a righteous look in her eyes, stood a little straighter, and said, "Let's go right now and tell the convention officials."

They looked around the lobby. People were chatting, removing their shoes, eating potato chips, and drinking cokes. One person held up her turtle shell so her friend could see it. Monica didn't see anyone with a badge and clip board.

"Where are all the officials?"

"Probably home. They're tired." Leslie yawned.

"I see some problems in our plan," said Monica. After we find the officials, we have to convince them charming John Spenser is a fraud. What proof do we have? Passing around a collection basket wasn't part of the convention rules, but he could argue he didn't know. The money? He could say the money is for African relief. And, of course, he would deny the entire conversation we overheard. The only hope we have is the honest indignation on our honest faces. Is that enough?"

Monica looked at Leslie who just shook her head. Their eyes exchanged the message honest faces wouldn't do it. As they stood watching the droves of unofficial people, Monica said, "We need to think like Nancy Drew, Miss Marple, or Jessica Fletcher. They wouldn't go home and crawl in bed; they would investigate. Let's wander back to the ballroom and check out the box with the water bottles."

Leslie scowled at her friend and shrugged her shoulders. "Why bother?"

"I could find evidence. Also, I'm just plain nosy," admitted Monica.

"I'll wait for you on this comfy sofa."

As Monica sauntered to the back of the empty ballroom, she tilted her head from side to side to see if anyone was watching her. When she got to the spot with all the equipment, she saw a box with several water bottles sticking out of the top. She deliberately dropped her sun glasses on the floor. To pick up her glasses would be a natural reason for bending down, just in case someone was watching. After another furtive peek over her shoulder, she poked around in the box where she discovered an empty vodka bottle.

Monica chuckled to herself. The old boy was indeed drinking while speaking. She wondered about the proportion of vodka to water and even had a moment's temptation to slip one of the bottles in her purse. A funny looking X on two of the bottles looked a little odd. She felt she shouldn't linger any longer so she grabbed her sun glasses and walked out of the ballroom into the lobby.

Leslie joined her in a few minutes. "What did you find out?"

"There's an empty bottle of vodka along with three water bottles. Two had X's on their tops. Weird. Do you think John's an alcoholic?"

"Probably, although he didn't stagger or slur his speech."

"Let's have a drink at the bar in the restaurant, and maybe we'll come up with an idea about what to do with the dishonorable peace guru," suggested Monica.

They headed for the dimly lit Black Cat restaurant and bar. The decor included black cats on the walls and black cat candle holders on each little round table. They sat down, ordered a couple beers, and groused about the situation. Since hungry people had to walk through the bar to get to the dining tables, they could easily spot John or an official.

Just as they were about to give up the chase and go home, John Spenser and Randy strolled into the bar. Randy had changed her clothes and wore black heels with lots of straps and a short, black skirt with a clingy pink blouse. The two went straight to the dining room where the hostess seated them immediately.

"Jessica Fletcher would take advantage of this opportunity," said Monica as she watched the two studying the menu.

"Maybe she would, but what would you do?"

"I don't know. We don't have much experience. Teaching school has restricted our adventurous spirits. Even Nancy Drew, the girl detective of the 50's, would do some thing."

For several moments, Monica contemplated her lost gumption. "I'll walk by their table and listen to their conversation."

Leslie put a damper on the idea. "You're going to look really odd. You walk into the dining room, tell the hostess you don't want a table, and just saunter over to the big fake's table, and stand there with your ears cocked like the dog that heard his master's voice. Real smooth."

Monica sighed, "Nothing is working out." They ordered another beer and munched on a few peanuts. " I know this will sound a little pushy, but what if I go directly to their table, give him another piece of paper with my cell number on it, and say something to the effect he might want another number."

"Weird."

Undaunted by Leslie's response, Monica stood up and strode over to the dining room. She speeded up to avoid the hostess's eye and went directly to John's table. Two pairs of surprised eyes stared at her.

"Hello, remember me? I'm Monica Walters, and I just want to give you my cell phone number in case you can't get me at home and want to make arrangements to speak to my students, and you need to phone me and sometimes it's difficult to find me, and so I thought I'd give you my cell number," stammered Monica. In her mind, she beat herself up for speaking again in a long run-on sentence.

Randy responded first. After giving Monica a tight little smile, she took the paper, and in a frigid voice said, "Thank you." A few seconds went by. Silence.

Monica wet her lips and asked, "Mr. Spenser, are you going to stay in Albuquerque for very long?"

"For about a week," he replied. He turned the corners of his lips up in a sort of half smile and continued, "I do have some appointments which will keep me busy, but I'll certainly keep you in mind."

His words dismissed her, but she plunged on. "I was hoping you could talk about civil disobedience in connection with the play *Antigone* my students are currently reading."

"Wonderful play. These modern playwrights have a great facility in expressing today's concerns. I would love to talk about the play in connection with my work, but I just don't know if I'll have the time."

Monica thought it would be so much fun to correct his literary blunder. She would love to point out his ignorance by saying Sophocles wrote this play 500 years before Christ was born; however, good manners prevailed. If she wanted to get more information out of him, she would have to act friendly. So she just smiled and said, "It's a great play. Good night."

When Monica returned to her table, she gleefully told Leslie about John's pretending to know *Antigone*. They chuckled and enjoyed his ignorance enormously.

"And another thing, they were drinking a bottle of Chanteauneuf du Pape. Let's look on the wine list and see what it costs."

Leslie grabbed the wine list and ran her eyes down the selections. "It's a $89 bottle of wine! And I paid for it." Her voice trembled. "That cad just bought an expensive bottle of wine with my donation. It curdles my stomach. His crimes have no limit."

Grateful she hadn't put much money in the basket, Monica knew it wouldn't be good to mention her wisdom at this time.

While Monica stared at the big phony's table, an attractive, young, college student in jeans and a tight blue tee shirt walked into the restaurant and went over to John's table. Her reddish hair, gathered into a pert pony tail, bobbed up and down as she nodded in an approving gesture to what John was saying. He stretched out his arm, indicating with his hand, she should sit with them. She cast a worshipful look in return.

Monica and Leslie unabashedly watched this drama. Randy continued eating her steak and occasionally sighed loudly. They couldn't hear what John was saying, but it appeared he was urging Miss Pony Tail to stay and have dinner with them. At first she shook her head back and forth, then smiled broadly, and nodded in apparent acceptance of his offer.

The waiter returned and took an order from Miss Pony Tail who beamed at her benefactor who in turn basked in the radiance of her adoration. Randy's eyes twitched while she stuffed a bit of baked potato into her mouth. She extended her arm and stared at her watch before she gulped down an entire glass of wine.

Monica and Leslie kept their eyes glued on John's table. After a few minutes passed, Randy looked at her watch again, picked up her purse from the floor, and poked around in it. Since she didn't remove anything, Monica thought she was just frittering away time while John impressed the girl with his magnificence. When Miss Pony Tail spoke, Randy yawned and John leered.

The drinking of the wine, the fidgeting in the purse, the minute by minute checking of the time must have become tedious because suddenly Randy stood up, spoke briefly to John and left, just a little short of a huff.

"What do you think happened?" asked Monica grinning maliciously.

"The same as you," answered Leslie. They giggled at the predictability of the situation. Later, a waiter brought in another steak dinner which Miss Pony Tail attacked. John poured more wine. Monica hoped Randy might appear again and more drama would take place.

Instead of Randy, a man in a suit walked over to John and whispered in his ear. John jerked his head and bellowed loud enough so Monica could hear clearly. "What? Are you sure? It can't be!"

He threw his napkin on the table, signaled the waiter he wanted his check, and said to Miss Pony Tail, "I've got to go. Jeff is dead!"

2

The ambulance was parked in front of the hotel, and two paramedics pushed a gurney with a sheet covered body through the lobby to the door. Wide-eyed people asked each other, "What happened?" "Do you know who he is?" "Poor soul!" Monica and Leslie were among the onlookers gathered to watch this somber ritual of removing the body.

"Jeff appeared to be a perfectly normal, healthy man just this afternoon. Now he's dead. It's so hard to believe," Monica said as she along with everyone else watched the gurney on its path to the ambulance.

Leslie repeated, "I can't believe it either. We just saw him."

In a corner of the lobby, a small group of employees gathered around one of the maids who was telling what she had seen. The maid had her head in her hands and was swaying slightly back and forth as she told her story.

Monica, carried away with curiosity, joined the group so she could hear the news. The maid rattled off her story without a pause. "I went into Room 354 with clean towels, and there on the floor was a man and near him was a water bottle and spilled water all over, and he had been vomiting greenish foam, and he looked kind of green in the face too, and it was a terrible mess, and I don't know what happened, but I think he was poisoned." The maid clutched her apron and gave it a couple of twists in her nervousness.

Monica scooted back to Leslie with the dire news. After relaying all the details, Monica made a solemn pronouncement, "Murder, most foul!"

"You don't know that. He probably died of some fatal stomach disease. You've been reading too many mysteries and watching too many episodes of *Law and Order*. People don't get murdered in nice hotels in Albuquerque. Just drug dealers and gang members murder each other, and they usually do it with guns or knives in cheap motels or dark streets. Honestly, Monica, you're over dramatizing his death," added Leslie.

"The maid said she thought he was poisoned," snapped Monica in defense of her conclusion of murder.

The two women continued watching the paramedics as they opened the ambulance door and slid the body into the back. Since the show was over, people began to leave the lobby. "I wonder when the police will arrive?" asked Monica.

"Why should they if he died a natural death? You're usually the sensible one, but now you've letting your imagination take over."

"You've said that before," Monica mumbled in a disgusted voice as she crossed her arms over her chest. A minute later her voice perked up, "Let's go up to Room 354 and check it out. Miss Marple, I'm sure would want to see the scene of the crime with her own eyes. The police aren't here yet, and after they come, they'll seal off the room and won't let us near it."

"If he died naturally, the police won't come. The room is probably locked anyway. I know you're going to go up to that room if I go or not. I might as well go along. Not every friend would play along with your crazy detective mania," said Leslie as they walked to the elevator.

"Thanks, I'm glad you're going with me."

"If the doctor is there, he'll probably just say Jeff died of a natural cause," repeated Leslie as they walked to the elevator.

"I'm tired of hearing he died of a normal disease. You need to have an open mind and consider other possible reasons for his death."

"Open mind? I need an open mind? Remember the insect energy bars," uttered Leslie as they entered the elevator.

The elevator stopped on the third floor. They walked down the hall and saw the open door to room 354. When Monica peeped in, she gazed at the grim scene where a man had died. Water had splashed out of a plastic bottle and made damp spots on the flowered carpet. Green tinged vomit had sprayed over a pillow, the bedding, and the floor. The brown bedspread was gathered in odd little bunches as if someone had grabbed handfuls of the soft material. As they looked at the scene of the crime, they stopped arguing about open minds.

"Icky!" said Monica.

"Yuk!" said Leslie.

"I pity the person who has to clean up this mess. Let's see if we can find a clue. If we walk on the other side, we won't step in the green stuff."

"I don't know if we should go in," Leslie said in a worried voice.

"Jessica Fletcher would go in," insisted Monica. "Nancy Drew would too, and she was just a teenager."

"But those are all fictional characters," argued Leslie.

"I'm going to do it," Monica said with spirit as she put her foot inside the door. Her eyes avoided the yukky stuff and concentrated on the bureau where a number of items lay in disarray.

Leslie stepped in too. "I hope we're not trespassing."

"Don't touch anything."

"I know that!" sputtered Leslie. "I watch TV."

Monica inspected the items on the bureau: keys, white handkerchief, leather wallet, a few coins, and a folded up piece of paper. She focused on the paper. "I think I found a clue!" She dug in her purse for a tissue which she used to cover up her fingers on the right hand. In an awkward way, she tried to unfold the paper by grabbing a corner and shaking it. The paper fell on the floor. She took out another tissue and covered her left hand thumb and fingers. While Leslie watched this unwieldy procedure, both tissues slid off Monica's hands. With an exasperated sigh, Monica bent down but couldn't pick up the paper with her bare hands.

Leslie came to her rescue. "Hold your hands out, palms up." Gently, Leslie placed a tissue on each extended palm and fingers. Monica slowly pinched the corner of the paper with her right hand and pinched the other corner with her left thumb and finger. With a tiny pull, the paper opened. The number 68 was written in black pen on the paper.

"I'm sure that's going to be an important clue," said the delighted Monica who carefully placed the paper on the bureau and folded it again without touching it once. "I think I should carry latex gloves in my purse so I'm always ready, although I don't remember Miss Marple or any of the other private eyes carried them."

While they stood facing the bureau, a voice came from the doorway. "What in hell are you doing here?" John Spenser glared at them. Monica's astonished eyes stared at a pair of menacing eyes.

John had his hands on his hips and scowled. Monica put her brain in fast forward and lied in her teeth. "The management asked us to check out Mr. Landsdon's room to see if he had any identification card with an emergency name or number on it."

John didn't speak for a moment as if he were mulling over this explanation. He smoothed the side of his hair with his right hand, forced a smile, and cleared his throat. "Of course, sorry I scared you. I'll give the information to whomever needs it."

"I'm very sorry about your loss, Mr. Spenser," said Monica.

"Yes, his death is a terrible blow to me. He was a friend as well as an invaluable employee. It's going to be hard for me to go on." He sniffed and brought a handkerchief to his eyes. "He probably died of a heart attack."

"If it was his heart, why did he vomit?" Monica asked.

"Sometimes people vomit when they have a heart attack." John didn't speak for a moment and then blurted out, " Unless he was poisoned from eating one of those insect energy bars!"

Leslie looked stricken. "Do you really think those bars are poisonous?" she squeaked.

"Could be, and if that is the cause, I'll sue!"

"Did he eat the tick one?" Leslie croaked.

"I don't know, but he and Randy were daring each other to eat one. I didn't pay any attention to what kind of insect. Why?"

"Well," gulped Leslie, "I ate one."

Monica wanted to reassure her friend and said, "The salesman has been selling those energy bars all weekend, and no one else has gotten sick."

"That's true. I haven't heard of any one else," Leslie said in a positive sounding voice.

Monica decided to change the subject. "Do you need any help with making arrangements. I know you're not familiar with Albuquerque, and I would be glad to give you information or whatever you need."

Leslie chimed in, "I'd be glad to help too."

"Thank you so much, ladies. I may call on you later," John said in a tone of dismissal.

The two women kept to the clean side of the room as they walked toward the door. At that moment an Albuquerque detective arrived with several uniformed officers. The handsome detective had a mass of black hair that spilled over his ears. He extended a skinny hand to the women and introduced himself, "I'm Detective Rick Miller. We heard Mr. Landsdon died very suddenly, and we were asked to investigate."

Monica and Leslie shook his hand and gave him their names. Monica knew they had to have an explanation for being in the room so she gamely said, "We came to help."

John now took over the conversation. "Nice to meet you, Detective. Jeff was my friend and employee. I had lunch with him and my other assistant, and we spoke together at various times during the afternoon. I am completely unnerved by his untimely death." John cleared his throat as if he were overcome with emotion.

Detective Miller took John aside while he continued to ask him questions. Monica felt left out, but she pulled Leslie's arm and guided her over to a corner of the room. "I have an idea. Maybe I could write a mystery about Jeff's death. I could even help Detective Miller find the killer. Miss Marple sometimes annoyed the inspector by being too nosy, but I won't do that. I can be discreet while at the same time manipulate the conversation so I can get some good information. Maybe he will even enjoy hearing my insightful deductions."

"You're crazy! He won't want to have anything to do with you, and besides you're still assuming Jeff was murdered." Leslie shook her head over her friend's misplaced enthusiasms. "I think reading all of Agatha Christe's mysteries has affected your judgement."

"I think it's possible I could work with the police. My cousin knows Detective Miller. In fact she used to date him after he got his divorce. She didn't date him for very long because she got interested in her personal trainer at the gym. Detective Miller is sort of scrawny, and my cousin likes the brawny type. I'm going to talk to him."

Leslie sighed and shook her head, "Whatever."

Monica's head was reeling with her opportunity to be part of the action and maybe even write about it. She waited until John had finished talking to the detective before she made her move. Casually she sauntered over to him and said, "I heard one of the maids say Mr. Landsdon was poisoned. Green foam does seem odd for a normal death, don't you think?"

"Poison? Tell me what you heard."

"Just idle gossip, nothing factual. The maid said it was murder." Monica shrugged her shoulders.

Detective Miller nodded and said, "Really?"

John Spenser broke into their conversation. "I want a thorough investigation of Jeff's death. This is an outrage!"

"We certainly will investigate. I'll send the water bottle to the lab, and the coroner will examine the body and determine the cause of death. I'll keep you informed, Mr. Spenser."

Monica piped in with an added comment, "I'm sure you'll check all the water bottles in case something was added to them, too."

John cast her a sharp glance. "You might find a little vodka since I occasionally need a little relaxer when I'm on stage." As he looked at Detective Miller, he grinned, winked, and tilted his head to show a you-know-how-it-is-with-us-boys look.

"Mr. Spenser, how much vodka do you put in each bottle?" asked Monica.

"I don't know exactly. I leave that to my staff. I have a high pressure position. It's not easy to be on stage in front of huge crowds of people. I do it because my message is important to the world. And what, dear friends, is more important than peace?"

Monica decided she should play along with him. She avoided Leslie's eyes since she didn't want to see her surprised expression. " Mr. Spenser, you are doing a wonderful thing by sending your message to the world."

John sighed and dropped his chin. Monica decided John probably had heard that line many times and knew how to react. He nodded with downcast eyes and conveyed to Monica the impression that although his life was difficult, he was doing it for the benefit of all people. Monica thought lowering his shoulders gave the impression he carried a huge burden and was a good gesture for fooling people.

When Monica looked up, no one was watching John. The policemen in the room were opening drawers, looking in the closet, and using tape measures. John walked away from the women, gave his card to a policeman, and left.

Although Monica wanted to hang around in case she might hear something important to the case, Leslie started guiding her to the door. They almost bumped into Randy who strode into the hotel room, tossed her hair, wiggled her nose at the mess, and backed away. "What happened?" she demanded. Her question didn't seem directed at anyone in particular, but Detective Miller went over to her.

Turning her head to whisper in Leslie's ear, Monica said, "Isn't it odd Randy isn't showing any sorrow. I noticed her thick mascara didn't ooze down her cheek, so she probably hasn't shed a tear. John didn't look upset either. Since all three of them travel and work together, I would think they would at least look depressed."

"Odd, very odd," replied Leslie. Randy was now seated and talking to Detective Miller. She flicked a piece of invisible lint off her skirt and crossed her legs, arched a foot enclosed in a four-inch heeled shoe, and checked her fingers for any chipped nail polish. Her eyes fluttered, and she dabbed at the corners with a handkerchief.

"Her mascara still isn't running, and it wouldn't take much to make it slide down," commented Monica.

Detective Miller moved across the room to talk with a uniformed policeman. Randy fidgeted with her bracelet while her eyes roamed. She stiffened her fingers to look for any chipped nail polish again.

"She's really worried about that polish. Her colleague just died, and she's probably wondering if she needs to call a manicurist," hissed Monica. "I'll give her my condolences and perhaps I'll get more information."

Monica stepped over to Randy's chair and said softly, "I'm sorry for your loss."

Randy looked up with knitted brows that had a who-in-the-hell-are-you look. But she smoothed the facial muscles to a tranquil mask and replied, "Thank you."

"I'm Monica Walters. I met you briefly when you were having dinner. Since I live in Albuquerque, is there anything I can do to help you?" Monica inwardly thought like giving you the name of a nail salon.

"Thank you, no. John will take care of everything."

"This must be a difficult time for you," Monica said sympathetically.

Randy blurted out. " I don't know what John and I are going to do. Jeff was the business man who took care of the finances, the scheduling, and the equipment. John and I are concerned about getting our message across to the people, so we don't know about all the details. Jeff joined us about a year ago when we really needed help. Our crusade had just taken off and scheduling conferences, finding hotels, and keeping the books were just too much for the two of us. Then he showed up."

"How did he happen to show up?" asked Monica.

"He contacted us when we were in New York, after we sent out an advertisement for an assistant. When we interviewed him, he said he could do everything so we could be creative and concentrate on the message. He was a godsend. He was nice, efficient, and good at his job. We'll miss him."

John reappeared at the door and went directly over to Randy. She put her hand on his shoulder and gave him a tight hug. He, in turn, hugged her back. John nuzzled her neck and kissed her. Monica stared unabashedly at this scene, but only for a moment because she heard a noise at the door. Miss Pony Tail, who had stuck her head in the doorway, was making yukky sounds. She stared at the vomit and wrinkled her nose in distaste.

John walked over to her and said, "I'm sorry, my dear, you saw this terrible scene. I hope you won't have nightmares. You're a delicate, lovely creature."

Monica heard Randy say under her breathe, "What about me? I'm not delicate and lovely?"

John put his arm around Miss Pony Tail's shoulders and turned her head aside so that she wouldn't have to look at the messy stuff.

Randy huffed a bit, barged in on the quiet conversation, and said in a frigid voice, "John, you need to introduce Jessica to the detective and the other two." Randy jerked her head in the direction of Monica and Leslie.

"So sorry, this is Jessica James, a student at the University, who is interested in our peace campaign," said John to the group as a whole. Monica and Leslie gave their names and shook her hand. The detective also politely acknowledged her.

John spoke in hushed tones to Jessica and explained, "This is a trying time for us. I know you didn't know the man. But we did. He was a friend and colleague, and we miss him"

"But I did know him," replied Jessica. "He worked on my campus crusade strategy. He told me my ideas were fabulous. Several of us have already collected money to send to Peace for Africa."

Now Detective Miller took interest and spoke directly to Jessica, "When did you last see him?"

"I saw him before John's lecture. He was in the back of the room with all the equipment. I didn't talk to him; I just saw him," said Jessica, formerly Miss Pony Tail.

Monica noted Randy's face stiffened when Jessica said, "John" and not "Mr. Spenser." It hadn't taken long for the college student to become familiar with her guru.

In a hearty voice John said, "Let's all go to the bar for a beer."

Monica poked Leslie in her side and whispered, "I think his offer includes us." With another jab, Monica pointed Leslie in the direction of the door. John strode ahead which left Jessica and Randy to follow. Before Monica took off for the bar, she rushed over to Detective Miller, put her hand half way over her mouth, and said, "I'll let you know if I find out anything."

Detective Miller had a bemused expression on his face. "Fine, I would be happy to get any information." He went back to his job, and John, along with the four women, headed for the bar.

3

The five of them sat down at a small, round table in a quiet corner of the Black Cat Bar. John ordered a pitcher of beer, leaned back in his chair, and exhaled deeply. Monica plunged immediately into asking questions about Jeff. "Was Jeff healthy in general? Have you noticed any behavior indicating he had a stomach problem or a heart condition?"

Shaking her head, Randy said, "He was healthy as a horse. He ran a couple miles every morning, ate burritos with hot chili sauce, and never complained about any aches or pains."

The waiter set the pitcher of beer on the table, and John poured each person a glass. "Let's have a toast." John lifted his glass and said, "To Jeff."

In unison the group said, "To Jeff." After the clinking of the glasses, they all took a pull.

Randy said, "We three had lunch together in the coffee shop just today. All of us ate hamburgers, fries, and cokes. So he couldn't have gotten sick from the hotel kitchen since we all ate the same things."

"What about snacks or other drinks?"

"Well, we did have a dare about one of those insect energy bars. Jeff ate it and won the bet," added Randy as she smiled briefly.

Leslie squeaked, "Was it the tick one?" Her eyes popped open wide.

"No, it was the grasshopper one."

Leslie exhaled slowly.

"We know he had a bottle of water, and it probably came from the box in the back with the sound equipment. We always have water available, but John has his own special water. We put a little black mark on the screw top in order to tell which bottles are his. You see, I hate water and vodka, and once I took one of his bottles by mistake and swallowed a big gulp. Ugh! The same thing happened to Jeff. Afterwards, we just made a little X with a ball point or whatever to make sure we wouldn't mix them up."

Monica perked up when she heard Randy mention the mark on the top. "Does anyone know if Jeff drank from a bottle with a mark on the top?"

John suddenly became animated. "I'm going to check on that," he said while getting up from the table.

Randy furrowed her brow and slowly asked, "Do you suppose there was poison in the bottle? Was he murdered?"

Monica nodded her head. "Yes, I think Jeff was murdered. Since he was a healthy man, he must have died from a poison, some sort of poison that gives off a green foam. The maid came to that conclusion immediately."

"But who would want to kill him?" asked Randy.

No one could respond to that question, so they all slammed more beer.

When John returned to the table, he mopped his forehead with a handkerchief and said in a hushed voice, "I found the bottle top in the waste paper basket. It had the X mark on it. If there was poison in the bottle, it was for me. I was the intended victim."

"Why did Jeff take a bottle with a mark if he hated the vodka-water combo?" asked Monica who was trying to think like the fictional detective, Stephanie Plum.

John tugged on an ear lobe as he thought about Monica's question. "Maybe Jeff took the bottle by mistake. He could have grabbed a bottle because he was in a hurry and didn't look carefully."

"Did anyone else know about the custom of putting an X on the bottle top to indicate it contained vodka?" asked Monica.

"Larry Gibbons works for me as a media consultant, and he knew about my little habit. I can't think of anyone else unless someone observed Jeff preparing the bottles."

"If he took a swig, you'd think he would spit it out or at least not drink anymore," said Monica. Another thought occurred to her. "Do you have any enemies? I agree you might have been the intended victim."

"My God, why in hell would anyone want to kill me? I stand for peace. The only person who hates my guts is my ex-wife, and she's in Arizona."

Randy said, "After the lecture, I walked back and saw three bottles in the box. Two had X's and one didn't. Why did he take a marked one?"

Leslie broke into their conversation, "At this point, we don't know anything for sure. He could have died from a natural cause."

"Be careful, John. I'm concerned about you," said Randy. Monica thought she truly looked concerned. She hadn't touched up her lipstick, which was worn away, or dabbed at a spot of beer on her velvet skirt.

During this conversation, Jessica hadn't said a thing. She just sat and nursed her beer, and every now and then she'd glance at John who wasn't paying any attention to her at all.

John was guzzling beer at a furious rate while mumbling, "I was the intended victim. What the hell! Why me?"

A stout man, wearing a rumpled shirt, came over to the group and croaked, "Geez, man what's going on? What happened to Jeff?" He sat down and drummed his fingers on the table. His round glasses and bushy brows gave him an owlish appearance. His fingers weren't the only active parts of his body as his shoulders twitched, and his knees bounced.

Everyone started to talk at once to explain the situation and the speculation. After a few minutes, John introduced him, "Larry Gibbons, my media consultant."

A waiter produced another glass and another pitcher. Larry grabbed the glass, poured the beer too rapidly so the foam slid down the side, and drank deeply. He kept mumbling, "Geez, man, I mean, is this really happening? Murder?"

Monica stared at the newcomer disdainfully. His stomach protruded over his belt. His stubby fingers never stopped thumping on the table, and his shoulders kept moving in funny spasms. All of these nervous twitches irritated her nerves. He didn't fit the image of the media consultants she had known who were sophisticated, suave salesmen. This guy could be a dropout from Hell's Angels.

Larry lit a cigar, took a couple puffs, and blustered away, "Lots of right-wing fruitcakes hate peace movements."

Lots of nods of agreement followed. "But," asked Monica, "how would these fruitcakes know about the X's on the bottles?"

Larry continued rapping his fingers and explained, "They're sneaky bastards."

Monica listened as everyone spoke of a case in which a celebrity had been killed by a fanatic who had spied on his prey and used all sorts of covert means to arrange the kill. When they had exhausted all references to deaths by psychos, they leaned back and drank more beer. Randy applied fresh lipstick, and Jessica reverted back to casting flirtatious looks at John. Larry cracked his knuckles and tilted his chair back on two legs.

Monica suddenly had an idea. "What about the vendors? Could one of them be a wacko who hates the peace movement?"

"No, I know many of them because they follow the conferences. They're out for a buck, nothing more. They do very well, too, which makes me think of selling my own tee shirts at these conferences. Any ideas about a logo?" asked John. Monica thought it was rather odd John could switch his mind to business so quickly after the death of his friend.

"How about a white dove with the word "peace" in capital letters and your name in small letters under it ?" Randy suggested.

"But a dove isn't manly," said John as he dismissed that idea.

"A big clenched fist with your name in all caps under it has lots of punch and testosterone," wheezed Larry.

"As a media consultant for the peace movement, do you really think a clenched fist would be a good logo?"

Larry shrugged his shoulders.

Leslie got into the spirit and suggested, "Perhaps a picture of you and Ghandi together with your names and something like 'We Work for Peace.'"

John shook his head. "Isn't he that little short, skinny guy? No, it'll spoil my image. But we have lots of time to consider the possibilities. Right now I have an announcement."

Leaning forward in his chair, John cleared his throat and spoke to the group in a loud voice. "This threat on my life by some deranged person isn't going to stop my crusade."

"You are sooo brave! Thinking of others while a cold-blooded killer is after your life. You're such an in-spiration." Jessica made a cooing sound as she praised his bravery.

John sat up straighter in his chair and repeated his heroic stand in a stately voice, "I will continue to work for peace no matter what danger there is to me."

Jessica said, "What courage."

Monica thought he certainly didn't want to end his income stream, but she, of course, wouldn't say such a blasphemous thing to these people who admired him. More talk erupted about the fact celebrities have to endure the curse of kooks preying on them. Jessica simpered about John's bravery again and again until Monica wanted to vomit. The evening came to a close. Jeff, the dear departed, had been forgotten as the living concerned themselves with their own lives.

After Monica got home, she could not stop thinking about the murder. She felt a compelling desire to find out who-done-it. She could be like Miss Marple and solve the crime before the police, which was an intoxicating and thrilling thought. The headlines in the paper would be "Teacher Cracks Murder Case, Police Astounded." She would write a best seller about the murder. Her students would listen to every word she said about semicolon usage, and the principal wouldn't bug her about getting her grades in on time. In general, her life would be rosier. She fell asleep while expanding on her grandiose idea of being Albuquerque's famous female sleuth and novelist.

4

"To investigate, I need to talk to the people who knew Jeff. But how can I do that?" Monica kept wondering as she graded papers. For days she had been trying to find a way. The police had an advantage, of course, because everyone expected them to ask questions. Finally, she decided to mask nosiness with a nobler trait, helpfulness. Quickly before she could chicken out, she called John Spencer at the Barclay Towers Hotel.

When he answered the phone, Monica said, "Hi, this is Monica Walters. I met you on the night Jeff Landsdon died. Would you like any help with making arrangements for his funeral or anything else?"

"Thank you for calling, Miss Walters. Just a moment, I'll ask Randy."

After a few minutes, Randy picked up the phone. "Yes, we need to know about crematoriums. Could you get some information for us?"

"I'll find out and call you back." After completing the call, Monica felt she had established a link to Jeff's friends. As Miss Helpful, she could ask questions, and no one would think she was being snoopy.

The next day, she felt bolder. Yesterday's conversations with John and Randy had gone so well. They were practically old friends now. Not only had they been pleased with all the information about the crematorium, but also with her contacts for the memorial service. She, in turn, hadn't found out much about Jeff, but she had gained their confidence.

Now, she dared herself to call Detective Miller. Before she lost her gumption, she tapped in the number for the Police Department on her cell phone. After asking for Detective Miller, she didn't have to wait long before he answered.

"Hi, this is Monica Walters. I met you at the hotel on the night Jeff Landsdon died."

"Miss Walters, I certainly do remember you. You were eager to help the police, and I appreciate that."

"Perhaps I'm being nosy, but I really am curious about the liquid in the bottle. Can you tell me what was in the lab report?"

"I suppose I can tell you since it will soon be public knowledge. The bottle from his room contained poison. The two bottles in the box contained both poison and vodka. An X was on top of each cap. Do you know anything about those X's?"

"Oh, yes," she answered eagerly. "I know the bottles with an X had vodka in them for John Spenser. He liked to have a little alcohol to relax him while he spoke on stage. The other bottles just had water. According to Randy, she and Jeff hated the vodka-water combination so they used the X to keep the two separate. Randy told me after the lecture, she walked back to the equipment area, and she saw three bottles: two with X's and one without."

"I find that very interesting since the bottle cap in the wastepaper basket in the hotel room had an X. I found no bottle cap without an X."

"Maybe she was mistaken," suggested Monica. "It's rather strange, however, because it would mean he deliberately took a bottle with vodka. Maybe he wanted a snort and decided to give vodka another try."

"I'll check with her."

"What was the poison?"asked Monica as she doodled a skull and cross bones on her scratch pad.

"A common one found in most insecticides that does not smell or have a distinctive taste," Detective Miller said.

"Which means anyone could have purchased the poison. I've heard access to poison is one of the trails investigators pursue when they're on a case. Isn't that right?"

"Yes, it is Miss Walters. You're really taking an interest in this case. Are you familiar with the people involved?"

"I don't really know them, but I helped them find a crematorium which has a little chapel for a memorial service. Jeff's only family is a brother in Alaska who isn't coming for the service so John and Randy made all the arrangements. The cremation is tonight, and the memorial service will be held on Saturday."

"Are you planning on attending? If you do, I'd appreciate it if you would tell me if you get any information that has a bearing on the case."

"Oh, I'd love to,"gushed Monica. "I'll go over there with the excuse I need to make sure all the arrangements are working out. I'll report back to you right away." Monica tried to sound like a cool, professional private eye, but she couldn't keep the delighted lilt out of her voice.

Immediately after she finished talking with Rick, Monica called Leslie. "Will you go with me to the crematorium tonight? Detective Miller actually asked me to report to him any significant information on the case I might hear. I had expected the police to be cold and formal, but instead this detective is nice, friendly, and rather sweet. It's almost like I'm working with him."

"I don't know much about how the police work a murder case, but I agree, he is treating you in a special way," said Leslie. "Sure, I'll go with you."

That evening Monica picked up Leslie in her Prius. They both wore jeans and Four Hills High sweat shirts. While Monica drove, she told Leslie the information about the poison she had gotten from the detective.

When they arrived at the crematorium, the parking lot was empty except for a Prius which Monica recognized as John's rental. Monica slid her car into the next space. Grass surrounded a plain stucco building with a large chimney. Off to the side was the chapel, a smaller building with a miniature steeple and stained glass windows.

The two left the car and walked into a vacant lobby area furnished with a plastic covered sofa, a dying potted palm, and several folding chairs. Monica recognized John's voice coming from an adjoining room.

"Let's get this thing over with. Where is the guy who lights the bonfire or whatever? I want to get out of this dump."

Larry's voice responded, "Geez, John, he'll be here. The money. I want my money. You said you'd have it by today. I've been waiting long enough."

In order to hear better, Monica tiptoed across the room, but Leslie sat down on the sofa. Monica unnecessarily put her finger to her lips as she cocked an ear in the direction of the voices.

"Don't worry, Larry. You'll get your money. I've been busy working on my eulogy. I just need a couple more days to get the bank account settled."

"Hey, you've been saying that for days!"

"I have more important things to think about than your money. The TV stations will probably be at the service tomorrow. In fact, there might even be national coverage. Too bad the chapel only holds about 50 people, but there's space enough up front for the guys with cameras. Randy, be sure you let them in first so they can get those front seats."

Monica heard Randy's voice. "John, remember to look stricken at all times. Those camera guys could catch you in an awkward pose, like looking bored. Those CNN teams can be all over the place."

"Do you really think CNN will come? I was hoping for CBS or NBC, but CNN would be great. CNN gets world coverage. I'll play the man who tries not to show his strong feelings, but at times lets his heart get through. Maybe a few tears, several sniffles, a sigh with a little catch in it. I've done that bit before, and it's quite effective."

"Forget the cameras. The money. Tell me when I'm going to get my money. What's to get settled at the bank? Just take it out and give it to me."

John's voice got a little softer, and Monica had to scoot closer to hear him. She was so interested in the conversation she risked exposure by almost putting her ear to the wooden door.

John explained to Larry in an exaggerated patient voice, "It'll all work out, but we have a little snag. Jeff put all the checks into an account called "Peace for Africa;" however, he died before I signed the signature card. His name is the only one on the account now. He told the bank I would come in and sign the card. As I said before, I should be able to draw a check on the account any day now."

"Yeah, yeah."

John's voice now had a business like quality. "We have a memorial service to worry about. I want both of you to wear something dark, not necessarily black, but something subdued. I'll wear my navy blue suit with a white shirt and dark tie. No, not white, but a light blue shirt since it might look better on TV. I've heard white washes a person out."

Randy's voice came through clearly, "I'm not going to wear a veil or even a hat. Veils aren't worn anymore. Jackie Kennedy was the last veil wearer I know of. I have a dark gray suit which might look nice with rose colored accessories. The blouse I wore in Cincinnati has a nice subtle light rose color that should be appropriate. I wouldn't want to wear a strong, bright red, but a delicate rose shade would make me look compassionate, besides being stylish."

"The dark blue tie with the blue shirt might be too much blue. Maybe I'll get a new tie," mused John.

"Geez," said Larry. "Forget the clothes. Just throw something on tomorrow. Nobody is even going to come to this funeral."

Monica got the inference that John disregarded the comment about no one coming to the service since he continued, "I've seen nice, silver toned ties at Dillard's which would look good with a blue shirt. I'll run over there and check out their tie selection. I read in the paper the store is open until 9:00 p.m."

"I'll go with you and look at shoes. I don't want to wear my heels with the straps since they are a little too sexy for a funeral. Maybe simple black pumps would look better."

Monica heard toe tapping and guessed it came from Larry's shoe. There were low mumbles which she couldn't understand. A door opened, and an unfamiliar voice came through quite clearly. "Gentlemen, and my dear lady, we have prepared your slumbering friend for his final good-bye. Would you like to observe the proceedings or shall I have the remains placed in an urn for your pick-up tomorrow?"

"Tomorrow morning will be fine."

Monica heard a door close and Larry's voice. "Hey, I want to see the bonfire. I've never watched anyone get roasted before."

"Larry, go on. Watch it. Follow the man."

A door opened and closed in the background.

Randy's voice spoke quietly, "What's all this non-sense about a snag in the bank account? You already signed the signature card."

"Yes, I know, but I need more time before I give Larry his money," answered John. "I have expenses here I need to pay first."

"Okay, okay. Let's get going to Dillard's."

Sensing the mourning group had ended the business of the night, Monica jumped back from her position of eavesdropping just in time as Randy and John opened the door that led into the lobby.

Monica rushed over to them and said, "I thought I would stop by and make sure all the arrangements are on track."

"Everything is fine, just fine. By the way, have you heard where the television crews are staying? I'm still at the Barclay Towers, and I haven't seen any," said John as he raked his fingers through his hair.

"No, but I could check it out for you. The local stations, of course, know about the memorial service, and I'm sure they'll come tomorrow. But I haven't heard whether NBC or CBS will be coming." Monica avoided Leslie's eyes.

"It's not that important, but if you do find out, I'd appreciate a call," added John. "I've had a terrible week, and the memorial service will be hard for me, but I'll persevere over all these ordeals." John inhaled deeply and looked down as if grief stricken.

Monica said, "The police have been making background checks on the participants at the conference, but so far they haven't found a likely suspect. I know you're concerned about another attack on your life," she said in a sympathetic voice.

"Yes, indeed. I no longer drink any bottled water. I buy canned sodas only. I wanted the local police to give me protection, but that Detective Miller told me they don't have enough men in the department to give me 24 hour security. So here I am, risking my life every day. No one knows what I've been going through," whined John.

He paused in anticipation of a comment about his bravery, but none came forth. Monica hated herself for sucking up, but she filled the gap of silence with a tepid exclamation, "You're so courageous."

While John studied his wringing hands, Leslie rolled her eyes and whispered to Monica, "You're so pathetic."

Monica gave Leslie a quick shake of her head in an effort to keep her quiet.

"Have you noticed if a particular person has followed you from city to city? There could be a stalker who knows your habits, particularly in connection with the water bottles. I've read in the newspapers about celebrities being followed across the country."

"I'll have to think about that. Usually I meet new people in each city, but, of course, it's possible someone has been stalking me. Randy, have you noticed any person who has repeatedly come to my lectures?"

Randy wrinkled her forehead and shook her head. "I don't remember anyone looking like a protestor. Of course, since most of the people wear jeans and tee shirts, it would be easy to blend into the crowd. A couple months ago we had a drunk cowboy who shouted out we were a bunch of communists. He might start a fist fight, but I doubt he would plan a killing which involved poison."

"There was a young man who came to the sessions here in Albuquerque. He sat in front and had his arms folded in front of him. As I recall, he had a scowl on his face and never even clapped once," John said.

"A non-clapping person isn't a strong suspect," Monica said. "I just had that random idea of a stalker, but obviously it wasn't a good one. I'm sorry I took up your time."

"I want to hear all ideas concerning my attacker. I have no faith in the police. They don't want to protect me, and they don't show any real concern over my safety. But I'll be strong." John coughed and cleared his throat.

After his brief bout of choking, he continued, "I'm paying for everything. Jeff was a good friend and employee, and I want to honor him in my modest way. Perhaps I'll scatter his ashes on top of Sandia Peak. He loved mountains and mentioned the view from the restaurant on the Peak was especially gorgeous."

"Did Jeff spend much time in Albuquerque before this trip?"

"I don't really know exactly, but he raved about the view from Sandia Peak a number of times. I've never been up there myself."

Randy chimed in, "He told me he had lived here for awhile when he was first married to Sheila. They moved to Chicago later, and then he started working with us. We all know Sheila, but I don't think he's still married to her anymore."

"The police have his address book so they could have contacted her. But if she was still married to him, she would be planning his funeral, and we haven't heard from her at all. They were always fighting and talking about divorce," added John.

"So you two are his closest friends," Monica said. "It's sad to think he has no family members to mourn him." Monica wanted to find out about his background although she didn't know if it would be valuable in the investigation of his murder. John's background, however, could bring something to light since he was the intended victim.

"Mr. Spenser, will any of your family be here to console you?" Monica asked while she twirled her necklace in a nervous gesture.

"No, I'll have to rely on my own strength of character. And, of course, my dear friends Larry and Randy are wonderful support." He smiled benignly at Randy, squeezed her hand, and took a quick peek at his watch. A door opened behind them.

Jiggling his keys, Larry reappeared and walked over to Randy and John. "Not much to see. Just flames through the glass panel."

"Yuck." said Leslie and Monica in unison.

Larry tossed his keys in one hand, Randy grabbed John's arm, and the three left. As the two women followed them out, Monica felt disappointed she didn't have much to report on the investigation. She'd call Detective Miller anyway and tell him what she heard.

5

Monica, dressed in a plain gray suit, stood with Leslie outside the crematorium on Saturday afternoon. People began appearing early for the 3:00 service. About 50 or 60 students carrying peace signs huddled together awaiting their guru. All the papers and TV stations reported that the police believed John Spenser had been the intended victim. Monica heard a few students voice the opinion he might not show because of the danger. These voices were immediately shushed as the others proclaimed that he was a brave man and would never hide from a perilous situation. The students sat on the grass, leaned on their signs, and looked down the street.

A skinny college student wearing camouflage pants and a baseball cap with its bill in the back entered the parking lot. He carried two wooden poles with cardboard signs which said, "Stop the Tyrants with War" and "War will keep us Safe from the Evil Ones." He took up a position opposite the peace students. Monica noticed the entire group had expressions of contempt on their faces probably because this brash intruder dared to defile their demonstration of love and harmony with a declaration of the benefits of strife. As he wagged one of the signs back and forth at an awkward angle, it slipped out of his hand and clattered to the ground. Monica watched from the side lines.

Jessica, now dressed in black pants and a white blouse, strode over to the protester. "Leroy, what are you doing here?"

"I'm protesting. Can't you see that?"

"Of course, I see that. This is one of the stupidest things you've ever done." Jessica put her hands on her hips and glared at him.

"I don't like the idea you're dating that old guy," whined Leroy.

"He is *not* old. He's just a little older than we are. And besides he's taken me to dinner twice at the Barclay Towers. You just take me to Taco Bell or McDonald's," added Jessica as she pursed her lips.

"I took you to the Olive Garden for your birthday."

"Big deal. You're going to spoil this memorial service. You're on the wrong side. Honestly, Leroy, you need to grow up. I like John, and I'm going to date him. And I don't care what you say or what you protest." Her gaze wavered from his face to something behind him. "Look, the Channel 13 news truck is coming and Channel 7 is just behind."

When Monica heard this, she craned her neck around to see the two news trucks pull into the parking lot. Everyone watched as the camera men got out their equipment, and the reporters grabbed their mikes. Leroy picked up his signs and waved both of his banners energetically in the air. Meanwhile the peace supporters waved their signs at him. The Channel 13 reporter immediately picked up on the situation and spoke into the mike, "We now have war and peace here in the parking lot of the crematorium without Leo Tolstoy in attendance."

A skinny, orange cat sauntered across the lot and rubbed its shoulders against Leroy's legs. The "Stop the Tyrants With War" sign drooped down and almost hit the cat. Leroy set it down and petted the cat's head. The war monger had a heart. The crowd said, "Ahh" in chorus. Both camera men zoomed in on this human interest event.

"Would you like to say a few words to our audience?"

"My name is Leroy Marx. I don't know where the cat came from, but he's really friendly."

"Yes, he's a friendly cat. But how do you feel about the peace campaign?" asked the reporter who held out the mike to Leroy.

"I think there's too much talk about peace. We should go in there and nuke those dictators."

"Oh, for God's sake, Leroy. You're just saying this for spite." Jessica said under her breath. "And I'm never going to speak to you again." She stomped off, and the newsman kept filming the cat.

John Spenser, who had arrived behind the two TV trucks, wasn't getting any coverage. Monica noticed he coughed several times as he walked to the chapel, but the cat and the kind hearted war advocate were upstaging him. Jessica looked from Leroy to John. After her huffing, she changed her expression to a sweet smile and walked rapidly over to John.

Leroy kept holding the cat while he talked to the reporter about nuking the bad guys.

At the chapel entrance, Randy was distributing light blue memorial cards with the deceased's name, birth and death dates, and a sentence that said, "He's at peace now." Although she spoke in a hushed voice to John, Monica was able to hear the words. "That was a great line for the memorial cards. It fits in so well with our theme."

Monica noticed John wore a navy tie with narrow silver stripes. She thought he must have gone to Dillard's last night. Randy was wearing pumps and not her heels with the straps so she, too, must have hit the mall. Both looked properly attired for a funeral.

John whispered back to Randy, "Be sure you let in any camera men. The reserved seats in the front are for them. I'll be sitting on the stage next to the table with the urn while the minister does his prayer thing. My eulogy should take about 20 minutes, the minister will say a prayer, and we'll finish up with a peace chant."

Randy gave a big sigh and mumbled, "I know, I know. We've gone over this a hundred times." John shrugged his shoulders and tugged at his tie.

Monica looked over at Leroy whose banners were on the ground since he seemed more interested in the furry, orange ball than promoting his agenda. After filming the cat, the newsmen returned to their trucks. As Monica peered more closely, it appeared Leroy was feeding the cat peanuts from his jacket pocket.

Monica who loved animals could no longer restrain herself. She walked over and said to Leroy, "I love cats, too. He looks like he hasn't eaten for awhile."

"Poor little thing. He's even eating my peanuts. That's all I have for him."

Monica put her hand out so the cat could sniff her fingers. His tongue gave her a couple of raspy licks. "What a sweet cat."

"Would you take him or find him a home? I live in the dorm, and we can't have pets."

Monica picked him up and felt his ribs as she held him. The poor cat was starving. No one could leave a starving cat. She'd take him home tonight and look for a home for him tomorrow. "I'll take him," she said to Leroy.

"Good, I'm glad I won't have to worry about him. I have enough stuff to worry about. That old guy stole my girl." With his head down, Leroy plodded across the parking lot dragging his banners behind him. The supporters of peace clapped.

While holding the cat, Monica walked back to the entrance of the chapel where Leslie stood talking to Randy and John. She told them the boy with the war banners had said, "The old guy stole my girl."

"I don't believe he's the killer type even though he has a motive for getting rid of you," Monica joked, as she looked at John.

"He said 'old guy' when he referred to me? What's wrong with that kid's eyes? I can't believe he said 'old guy.'"

"Well, he's just a freshman," Monica said as if that could take the sting out of the abusive word.

John turned to Randy. "Do I look old?"

"Of course not," she said quickly.

Monica and Leslie both added, "You look very young." Monica felt she wasn't telling a lie, just exaggerating a little bit. John looked somewhat relieved.

Randy checked her watch. "We've got to get started. We're already 15 minutes late. We've held the service up long enough, and it's time to get things rolling, cameras or not." She signaled to one of the funeral employees to start the music, and the service officially began.

Because she was still holding the cat, Monica stood in the back with Leslie. After the opening prayer, John walked to the podium with slow, measured steps. His beautifully controlled voice oozed sadness. "My friends, we are here to give homage to my close friend who died for me. He drank the poisoned cup that was supposed to be mine. Even though a cold hearted killer wants to stop my work, I will continue my crusade for peace."

"I think I know what the main emphasis of this eulogy will be," whispered Monica.

Leslie agreed. "His great love, himself."

"I'm worried about this little cat. Leslie, you should stay in case something happens," said Monica with just a hint of optimism. "I'm going to Walgreen's and buy some cat food. I'll be right back."

When Monica returned, she left a sleeping orange cat on the passenger seat of her car. The hungry cat had eaten about a half cup of Meow Mix and drank a paper cup of water. Feeding the cat cheered up Monica. A little, starving animal needed more attention than an ego maniac. Monica slipped in the back of the chapel and tapped Leslie on the shoulder. They both left quietly.

As soon as they could speak privately, Monica asked, "What happened?"

"Both newsmen from Channels 13 and 7 filmed John during an emotional moment when his shoulders were hunched and shaking in the midst of a sobbing episode." Leslie added, "John emphasized the poisoned cup Jeff drank for him." Monica wondered if John had been a theater major in college.

Outside, everything appeared to be very calm. The peace supporters were sitting on the grass and talking quietly while they waited for an audience. Monica and Leslie also waited outside for the service to end when Larry ambled over to them. He came from the parking lot and walked in his typical nervous fashion. One shoulder jerked up and down, and his fingers on both hands clenched and unclenched. "Service not over yet?" he asked.

"It should be over soon, " replied Monica.

"Couldn't make it. Had important business to do. But I'll miss Jeff ."

A tall, blonde woman came from the parking lot. She wore a navy blue suit, navy heels, and carried a huge tote. She rushed over and asked, "Is the service over? I just flew in from Chicago, and the plane was delayed. I'm Sheila Landsdon, Jeff's wife."

Monica and Leslie introduced themselves, but Larry already knew her.

Larry said, "Hi Sheila, nice to see you. I really didn't think you'd come. I thought you and Jeff had divorced."

"I filed, but the divorce isn't final." She set her big tote on the ground and two little furry faces popped out of the top. "These are my Yorkshire terriers, Rhonda and Stephanie. They are such good companions. I take them everywhere with me. Jeff never liked them, although he was gone so much of the time he hardly knew them at all."

"I'm sorry you missed the service," said Monica.

"I don't care about any service. I hope to collect some money," answered Sheila.

Monica thought that here is an honest person. No false sympathy from her.

"I don't want to sound heartless, but I don't really miss him. He was playing around with other women on all those trips he took with that big fake, John Spenser. So why shouldn't I get a little something for those years I spent married to the jerk."

No one answered her. Making money on the death of a wayward spouse didn't seem to be so bad thought Monica.

Larry asked, "Is there a will?"

"Oh, I have the will. He made it out five years ago when we married. I'm the sole beneficiary. He has a brother in Alaska, but he hasn't seen him for 20 years or more. I don't know where he banked or how much money there is. Jeff was always so tight with me. Do you know where he took me on my birthday? The Olive Garden."

Monica thought the Olive Garden wasn't a good choice for birthday dinners.

Sheila continued, "Rhonda and Stephanie are such good travelers. They slept on my lap for the entire plane trip." While she was talking, the dogs were busily dancing between people's legs and wiggling their silky tails. Sheila bent down and petted each little head. "I don't know why Jeff hated the dogs. He was really quite unreasonable."

Randy had the entrance door ajar and took a brief look inside. "It's almost over. John is making his final comments. Sheila, would you like to slip inside?"

"Maybe for a moment." Sheila opened the door a little further and went into the chapel. Before anyone realized what was happening, two small dogs ran into the chapel at the heels of their mistress. They scampered up the aisle and emitted joyful little barks. The eyes of all the members of the audience were on the two dogs which were pausing now and then to sniff the outreached hands of some of the animal lovers. A few people started to giggle. John was upstaged again.

One person, who was seated on the aisle, told either Rhonda or Stephanie to sit and then produced a dog biscuit. From the doorway, Monica watched this episode worthy of Animal Planet. She wondered if this person carried dog biscuits with her all the time. The other dog, noticing food was available, trotted over to the biscuit carrying person. Both little mop dogs sat and waved their tiny paws. It was a precious moment, and most people were smiling. Not John, however, he grimaced.

Sheila called out, "Rhonda, Stephanie, here!" They paid little attention to her and kept pawing the air as an enticement for more goodies. The woman with the seemingly endless supply of biscuits kept giving out more while murmuring to the animals in some sort of doggie talk.

Sheila said, "Sorry" to no one in particular, picked up the pooches, and walked out the door. Even after the dogs had been removed, the atmosphere still remained upbeat. John had lost control of the aura of tragic death. He quickly finished his eulogy and nodded to the minister that it was time to end the service. The minister bowed his head and prayed for Jeff's soul Most of the people followed his example, but a few still looked at the retreating dogs and smiled.

People spoke to John outside the chapel while his entourage stayed in a small group off to the side. Monica and Leslie continued to hang out with Randy, Larry, and the new addition, Sheila. Some of the mourners stopped to pet Stephanie and Rhonda. They ran around in little circles and enjoyed the attention. Sheila said to the group, "See how cute the dogs are. Everyone loves them. Of course, *he* didn't. *He* always complained about them."

Larry moved his weight from one foot to the other and snapped his fingers which the dogs interpreted as a command to come. They sat in front of him in expectation of good things, but Larry just looked at the dogs and didn't bend down to pet them. They increased their activity by sitting up and waving their little paws. This trick never failed, but Larry seemed clueless about what they wanted or else he really didn't care. He just kept moving back and forth while his fingers kept snapping, perhaps to the beat of some interior song.

Monica's love of animals made her come to the rescue of the frustrated Yorkies. She bent down and stroked each little head. Sheila smiled and said, "You obviously love dogs. Do you have one at home?"

"Yes, I have an old rescue dog and a cat. And just today I picked up an orange cat the war supporter befriended. He said he lived in the dorm and couldn't have a pet. I'm going to either find this cat a home or keep him. He's very friendly. Since my black cat at home is old, I don't know if she'll make a fuss. The dog won't care."

"I feel if they have enough love, it'll all work out," said Sheila.

Randy looked bored. Monica thought animal talk wasn't everyone's cup of tea although to her it was always interesting. John and Jessica now joined the group.

John spoke to Sheila, "I didn't think you'd come since you divorced Jeff."

"The divorce isn't final. I really came to find out where he kept his money since I have his will, and I'm the sole beneficiary. I probably sound mercenary, but he really was a lousy husband."

" I don't think he had any money. I hate to say it, but he was a spendthrift. He spent his salary almost the day he got it."

"Two months ago he boasted to me he was going to buy a new Mercedes and pay for it with cash. When I asked him how he got the money, he clammed up and mumbled he couldn't say. I thought he was up to something, but I couldn't get anything more out of him."

"I paid for the cremation and the memorial with my own money. If you find his bank account, I'll send you a bill," replied John.

Monica thought the lover of peace and suffering mankind certainly didn't miss an opportunity to get a little cash. Sheila didn't reply. She bent down, tucked the little dogs into their fleece pouch, and lifted the furry container to her waist. To Monica, Sheila looked like some sort of human kangaroo.

John's head drooped while he spoke softly to Randy. "CNN, CBS, ABC, none of them came. Just the Albuquerque stations. I guess I'm just not worth it."

Jessica, who linked her arm through John's, immediately made soothing noises. "Maybe there was a war somewhere."

Randy brushed back a lock of her hair and repeated Jessica's comforting words, "Some country probably attacked another."

John seemed to brighten a bit. "I bet that's it. A war started." He held up his head. "Let's all go for a drink." Everyone nodded except Sheila.

"Bye, all, I'll see you later," Sheila said as she turned and flipped her long blonde hair back from her face. She walked off taking long strides and holding her bundle of fur.

Monica whispered to Leslie, " I never forget a dog. I don't remember seeing Sheila, but I saw those two Yorkies at the Barclay Towers last week, the day Jeff died."

6

"Let's head for a bar. It's been quite a day," said John. He looked at Jessica and then at Randy. Monica wondered how he was going to manage the situation with two women. Jessica had already linked her arm through his in a possessive way, but Randy had a lot of experience with the showman and probably could outmaneuver the younger woman.

"All of you could come over to my place. My apartment is fairly close," said Monica. Everyone, except Larry, nodded as an indication that they liked the idea.

Larry mumbled, "Count me out." Still snapping his fingers, he walked off.

After Monica gave directions, Randy curled her hand around John's free arm, and the three of them walked towards the rental Prius while Monica strolled over to her Prius. Leslie followed behind.

When Monica opened the door, the cat didn't try to jump out. He just stretched his legs and yawned. Leslie picked him up when she sat down in the passenger seat. The cat settled himself on Leslie's lap and purred. "I bet you keep this cat. He's so loveable. You won't be able to part with him."

"You know how I love animals. I just hope my cat, Marilyn, and my dog, Mitsey, won't mind. You know how they can get jealous."

As Monica started her car, she craned her neck around to see what was happening to the incongruous trio. "Leslie, can you see them? I bet both of the women try to dart into the front seat as soon as he opens the door."

Leslie giggled, "Randy is the winner. She's snuggled up against John in the front seat while Jessica is alone in the back seat."

Enjoying this little drama immensely, Monica laughed as she drove. "Let's gossip. What do you think of Larry? He's just so weird. All he talks about is getting his money. Frankly, it doesn't sound like he's talking about a salary or a commission. I don't think he works for John."

"I agree Larry is weird. He makes me nervous with all his jerks and clicks. He's either 'on' something or he's crazy. Of course, he could be a gangster which means that he takes dangerous drugs and probably has a gun."

"Do you really think he carries a piece?" asked Monica with a touch of pride that she knew gangster lingo.

"Next time I see him, I'll try to bump against him or look for a bulge under his arm. But why does John owe him money?"

"Maybe gambling or blackmail. In all the detective novels I've read, gangsters are always using blackmail to get money. Also, it's possible Larry wants to collect on a gambling debt. John should be worried Larry could send in some goons to break his knees."

"I bet Randy knows what's going on. I"ll try to get some information for you," Leslie said while petting the cat.

"Good, you work on Randy, and I'll work on John. Too bad Jessica will be with us because she complicates things. She's always praising him until I want to gag," said Monica as she drove down Lomas Blvd. toward her apartment.

A few minutes later, they arrived at a white stucco apartment house with a couple of maple trees in the front yard. After Monica parked her Prius, the two climbed the outside stairs to the second story apartment. Monica firmly held the orange cat although he didn't try to escape from her cradling arms. When she opened the door, her dog ran to meet her. Mitsey gave a brief glance at the new cat and wagged her tail. Monica quickly walked over to her counter where she kept a bowl of milk bones and handed out a treat with one hand while the other hand clutched a scared, wiggling cat. Mitsey gobbled up her crunchy milk bone and walked over to greet Leslie with her nose twitching in anticipation of friendly pets.

Marilyn, the black cat, however, had a different reaction to the new cat. Instead of indifference, she was intensely interested. The hair on her neck stood straight up, and her tail lay flat on the floor and twitched occasionally. She hunkered down in preparation to spring.

Monica set the nervous kitty down on the carpet at the other end of the room away from Marilyn who kept glaring at the uninvited guest. Monica tried to appease Marilyn by petting her and saying, "You're the best cat in the entire world, and you should help out a poor homeless animal."

This sweet talk seemed to work since her hair settled down, and she slithered over to sniff the intruding cat that hadn't moved. More sniffing. No growling or hissing. A good sign. Monica set down a saucer of milk for Marilyn only. She lapped up most of it and leaped to the top of the sofa, but kept her eyes on the new cat that still didn't move. Monica started to feel optimistic about acquiring the orange kitty; she even rolled around a couple names in her head.

Since company was coming, Monica didn't have any more time to pursue the relationship between the cats. She took out a bottle of vermouth and a bottle of gin for martinis. After she had shaken—not stirred—the martinis, she checked her liquor cabinet for vodka. No vodka in the house. Although she knew John liked vodka, he probably wouldn't want it anyway, considering the past circumstances.

Leslie helped her get out a couple bottles of white wine, find the goblets, and put a square of cheddar cheese on a plate. Monica shook out some wheat thins and Ritz crackers into a couple of wooden bowls. The impromptu party wouldn't have many snacks, but probably everyone would be more interested in the booze anyway.

"Leslie, I'm doing too much multitasking. I'm trying to solve a murder, introduce a new pet to my little animal family, give a spontaneous cocktail party, and prepare a lesson plan on *Hamlet*." As she spoke, she was making an artistic arrangement of the napkins, the cheese, and the crackers on the coffee table.

"You've done *Hamlet* before so all you need to do is go over your notes. And the rest of the things will come together somehow," soothed Leslie.

As Monica set down the martini shaker, she glanced outside the window and saw a car parked in front. "They're here."

Monica opened the door to greet John, Randy, and Jessica who were getting out of the car. Off to the side, she saw a young man in camouflage pants standing under one of the maple trees. He was the bearer of war slogans and the cat rescue person.

Jessica shouted at him, "Leroy, stop following me! Your are *such* an idiot. I'm never going to speak to you again."

"But I love you!"

"You're a big fat idiot!" She put her hands on her hips while she ripped into him.

"I'm just a person in love." His chin twitched.

"Get out of here. You'll be late for your job," she snapped.

"I don't care if I'm late. I love you." He held his hands in a praying position while he professed his love.

John said to Randy, "That's the kid who didn't clap at my presentation. In fact, I told you about him.

He had a scowl on his face and crossed his arms in front of his chest like he resented every word I said."

Randy added maliciously, "I think he's also the one who referred to you as 'that old guy.'"

John narrowed his eyes and glared at Leroy. Standing at the top of the stairs, Monica shouted out to Leroy, "The cat's here."

Leroy switched from declaring his love to Jessica to concern over the cat. "How's he doing?"

"Fine, do you want to come up and see him?" Four pairs of eyes stared at Monica who interpreted their expressions as what-are-you-thinking-you-crazy woman.

To Monica's surprise, Leroy said, "Sure, I'd like to see him. And, Jessica, will you let me talk to you privately for a few minutes?"

Jessica didn't answer him at first; she just glared at him. " I'll give you a couple minutes, but that's all."

"I can't believe he's going to intrude on our party." Randy sniffed her disapproval.

While the group climbed the stairs, Monica fumbled around in her junk drawer to get out the wine bottle opener. She set it by the wine and made a quick glance to make sure all was in readiness. When she looked around the room, she didn't see the new cat or her own cat. She felt a little panic, but when she peered in the bedroom, she saw the two kitties snuggled together on the bed. Marilyn was licking the new orange one in a loving fashion.

After everyone had entered, Monica immediately took Leroy to the bedroom to see his rescued cat.

Jessica followed along. When Leroy saw the harmonious cats, he smiled and looked at Jessica. "They look like they're made for each other, just as we're made for each other."

"Leroy, you're going to be late for your job. You better go," urged Jessica who had lowered her tone considerably.

Monica noticed she hadn't called him an idiot again. Perhaps she was thawing a little. She, also, didn't end the conversation with the I'm-never-going-to-speak-to-you-ever-again line.

After Leroy had seen the tranquility of the rescued cat, he went into the living room where everyone had a drink. The women were sipping white wine while John chugged his martini, grabbed the pitcher for a refill, and stuffed a cracker with cheese into his mouth.

As a good hostess, Monica offered Leroy a glass of wine which he took. No one spoke. No one seemed to know what to say to this unwelcome odd person. Jessica focused her eyes on Leroy and repeated, "You need to go to work, or you might get fired."

Monica's curiosity was aroused. "Where do you work?"

"I work at Morgenstern's supermarket. I'm the person who hands out pastry samples. The baker has a new butterscotch cake with chocolate drizzled over the top. I cut each cake up and put little pieces on napkins so the shoppers can taste the new cake. People just gobble up the samples. Most of them buy a cake after they've tasted it." After his lengthy explanation, he confessed a small glitch. " I got in trouble the other day because I let the carry-out boys eat samples. The manager doesn't like that."

"Leroy, you have a good job. You better not goof it up. I'll talk to you later." Monica thought Jessica was giving Leroy some hope.

Leroy slammed down the wine, smiled at Jessica, and said, "Thanks." He left, presumably to head out for his job.

"Butterscotch cake with chocolate. Yummy. I think I'll make a trip to Morgenstern's place myself," said Leslie. Everyone nodded.

"Someone who hands out butterscotch cake with chocolate and likes cats can't be a murderer," Monica said.

John, who had poured himself another drink, muttered, "Damn kid, you never know what goes on in someone else's head."

Jessica piped up, "He's such an idiot. He's just a big, fat idiot." She stood up and headed for the bathroom.

Monica thought she had better try to get things off these side tracks and concentrate on solving the case. She sidled up to John who was now gulping his third martini. "Have you noticed any strange behavior from anyone lately?"

"No, but celebrities, as we have discussed before, have problems with kooks. That kid is odd although Jessica seems to know him. I'll be glad when this week is over, and I can leave. I promised Jessica I would speak at several gatherings this coming week. College students are enthusiastic about peace. Their idealism is a beacon of hope for the world."

A knock on the door stopped everyone's conversation. When Monica opened the door, Detective Rick Miller, wearing a white shirt with a tie, stood in front of her. "Pardon me for intruding," he apologized, "but I was late for the final rites, and I heard a few people had gone to your house for a wake. Would you mind if I joined you?"

Monica was terribly impressed the detective had come to her apartment. Secretly she thought he was cute, although scrawny, and he had all sorts of information about the murder scene she wasn't privy to.

"Please come in. This is an informal gathering," she said. Introductions weren't needed as everyone had spoken to the detective earlier. He didn't take an alcoholic drink, but sipped on a coke and munched a few crackers.

Randy immediately asked, "How is the investigation going?"

"We don't know who did it yet, but we're still gathering information. Do any of you know something you might think is insignificant but actually could be important?"

"I think Larry is a gangster," blurted out Leslie. "Monica and I both think so."

Monica gave Leslie a disgusted look and tried to explain, "He looks like a criminal, and he keeps demanding money. To me, that's suspicious."

"We should have you on the staff," chuckled Detective Miller. "You could save us a lot of time." But his face changed from the humorous notion of identifying criminals from their appearance to a serious question.

"Why does Larry owe you money?" asked the detective looking at John.

John cleared his throat, downed another big swallow of martini, and said, "It's a matter between the two of us."

"He doesn't work for you?" asked Monica who suddenly became emboldened.

John poured his fourth martini, raked his hands through his hair, and mumbled, "No, he doesn't."

"Is it a gambling debt?" Monica kept on grilling him.

Everyone waited for his answer. "Well, ahhh, yes," he croaked softly.

"Do you gamble?" blurted out Jessica as her eyes got wide.

"Just this once. I took this first ever bet on the Nebraska-Oklahoma game. I thought the Cornhuskers would win by a big margin, but they lost. I only made the bet to help out the Peace for Africa movement. I would never have done it for my own gain." As John ended his confession, he gave Jessica a sloppy smile.

Randy rolled her eyes and reached for the martini pitcher.

"How much do you owe him?" persisted Jessica.

"One hundred dollars. I bet on Nebraska, but those Cornhuskers lost. But as I said before, this was my first bet, and I've learned my lesson. I'll never do it again," he promised.

"It takes a great man to admit a mistake," said Jessica as she gave him a worshipful look.

Randy appeared to get something caught in her throat, sputtered a bit, and did another eye roll. Detective Miller put his hand over his mouth like he was going to stroke his chin, but Monica noticed he was covering up a grin.

Jessica looked at John. "I'm so glad to hear you won't gamble again. To lose one hundred dollars is a lot of money, but I know you really had your heart in the right place. You're just trying to help those poor Africans. I'll try my best this week to help out your movement."

Monica wanted to do an eye roll, but she was facing the group. Instead she looked at the detective and asked, "Does Larry have a sheet?" She loved using cop talk. After watching *Law and Order*, she felt she knew all sorts of inside expressions.

He nodded, "Yes, but that's all I can say."

"Did you know Larry was a criminal?" blurted out Jessica as she focused her eyes on John.

John proclaimed his innocence, "No, this is a surprise to me. I had no idea he had been arrested. I'll just pay him the money and never see him again." Monica was amazed at his spontaneous fiction. He kept dishing it out, and Jessica ate it up. Monica assumed no one else believed what he was saying.

"Where is Larry now?" asked Detective Miller.

"Are you going to arrest him?" asked Randy.

"No, I'm just curious."

Monica heard his denial, but she thought that could be what the police always say. Larry might be "on" something illegal, and the police might be tailing him. All those jerks and spasms might not just indicate a very nervous person but could be due to drugs which would fit in with being a criminal.

At this point, John and Randy looked at their watches. Almost in unison they said, "It's getting late. We better go." John grabbed Jessica by the arm, mumbled thanks, and stumbled out the door. After four martinis, John could still talk without slurring his words, but he swayed back and forth in a hazardous fashion. Randy, who was directly behind him, grabbed his arm to keep him upright.

"I should go too. I have papers to grade," said Leslie as she followed the others down the stairs. Now Monica just had one guest.

Detective Miller didn't seem in a hurry as he sat back in his chair and pushed back some hair that had drooped over his forehead. "You're really taking an interest in this case, aren't you? By the way, let's not be so formal. Please call me, Rick."

"And I'm Monica." She paused after that shared bit of intimacy. "I am interested in this case. If I could solve this murder, I could use it as an inspiration for my own writing."

"You know, I've never met anyone like you before. You previously said you were an English teacher. That was my favorite subject when I was in high school."

"Oh, really," murmured Monica. "I teach English 12, and tomorrow we're going to start *Hamlet*. Have you read it?"

"Yes, it was one of my favorites." Rick set his coke glass down on the coffee table.

"In general the kids like it, and they agree with Hamlet his mother shouldn't have married his uncle so quickly after his father died."

" I felt the same way when I read the play. I still feel starting a new marriage a short time after the death of a spouse is too soon," said Rick.

"*Hamlet* is like a contemporary detective story. Hamlet hears from his father's ghost that his murderer is the current king, his uncle. Hamlet uses various methods to get proof of his uncle's guilt. He doesn't want to take vengeance on just the word of a ghost. That's like the modern method of using clues to figure out who committed a murder or a crime. I like reading about this process, and you must enjoy actually taking part in solving real life crimes," commented Monica as she let her eyes focus on his eyes.

"Yes, I do, but this current murder has me baffled, and I'm not enjoying the idea a killer might get away with it."

"The only person who has shown some dislike to John is that kid, Leroy Marx. I can't believe he's capable of such a thing," said Monica as she reached for a cracker.

"Jealousy is a motivator, but I agree with your sensitivity about people. He doesn't seem the type," said Rick. "I'm going to talk with him a little more.

Do you want to come with me to Morgenstern's store and sample some butterscotch cake with chocolate drizzle?"

Monica was touched that Rick, no longer Detective Miller, wanted her to go with him. "Sure, I'll just check on the cats, and I'm ready." When she looked in the bedroom door, the two were sleeping with their noses touching. She thought she'd keep the rescued cat and call him Bob.

As Monica walked out with Rick, she felt excited she was actually taking part in police work. Things were working out.

7

Morgenstern's store was in the strip mall near the University of New Mexico. This huge supermarket catered to the entire city, in addition to the University community. Monica and Rick walked directly to the bakery area where the smell of fresh bread filled the air.

Leroy Marx, dressed in a white shirt and a long waiter's apron, stood behind a small table with samples of cake on little napkins. His large weave hair net gave him a pathetic appearance. A younger kid, probably about 16, was eating cake and talking to Leroy. As Monica and Rick approached, the kid reached for another sample. Monica thought that probably one of the bag boys was on break.

"Hello, Leroy," said Rick.

"Hello, Detective Miller and Miss Walters. Would you like to try our new butterscotch cake with chocolate?" Leroy pointed to the little squares on the table.

Each picked up a napkin that held a portion of cake, took a bite, and made yummy sounds. "I could eat an entire cake; it's so delicious," said Monica as she licked her lips.

"I'll buy you one," said Rick as he selected one of the boxed cakes stacked on the side of the table.

"Gee, thanks. I get credit for all the cakes I sell," said Leroy as he shifted his weight from one foot to the other.

"By the way, Leroy, how long have you known John Spenser?" asked Rick in a friendly manner as he flicked crumbs off his fingers.

"I don't really know him at all. He stole my girl. He came on campus and talked to the students about peace and all that stuff. Peace, I suppose, is okay at times, but you need to get rid of those tyrants by bombing them off the face of the earth. Jessica thought he was wonderful, and then she went to that conference and started dating him. Can you believe she's dating that old guy? Now she won't give me the time of day." His head drooped as he spoke.

"Did you go to his lecture on Saturday, the day of the murder?"

"Yeah, I went. It was disgusting. A bunch of girls from school ran after him to get his autograph and gush over every word he said. And Jessica , she was the worst of all. She kept saying how wonderful he was."

"Did you know Jeff Landsdon?"

"No, I never met the dead guy." At that point another shopper reached out for a sample, and another bag boy cadged one on the sly. Monica thought Leroy didn't seem to know much. She hoped they would leave soon since the cake corner was getting busy and wasn't a good place for conversation. Detective Miller waved good-bye to Leroy and carried the cake to the check out. After he paid for his purchase, he handed it over to Monica.

"Thank you, Rick, you'll have to come over and help me eat it." Rick grinned and nodded. Monica noted he had a nice, boyish smile. They walked out the door while discussing the unseasonably warm weather for fall and the good football game that the Lobos, the University team, had played over the weekend. Just easy, pleasant conversation.

As they were getting into the car, Monica turned her thoughts to the case. "Have you spoken to Jeff's ex-wife? She said she just arrived today, but she was here last weekend, on Saturday, the day Jeff died. I know she was at the Barclay Towers because I saw her Yorkshire terriers. And I never forget a dog. I know all the dogs in my neighborhood, but not their owners."

"Really, I haven't met her yet." Rick perked up when he heard the news.

"She came late to the memorial service. When I talked to her, she said she was the sole beneficiary of his estate since the divorce wasn't final. I think she hoped to come into some money since she said Jeff bragged to her he was going to buy a Mercedes with cash." Monica hoped the information had some relevance.

"Umm," said Rick thoughtfully.

"She probably knows a lot about John, too. Jeff probably told her stuff about his boss. Ex-wives are a good source of dirt, as you know, of course." She gave him a flirtatious smile.

Rick smiled back and nodded. "Yes, indeed. I'm going to have a little chat with her. Would you like to come along?"

Without missing a beat, Monica blurted out, "Of course."

The two of them chatted about the fun and challenges of teaching high school as they drove to Barclay Towers. When they arrived at the hotel, they saw a lady with two Yorkshire terriers walking out of the hotel door. "That's Sheila," said Monica.

Monica leaned out of the car window and shouted, "Hi Sheila, Detective Miller is with me, and he'd like to talk to you about Jeff."

"I'll be glad to tell him what I know about that jerk and his scheming boss," replied Sheila. "Let's sit at a table outside in the shade since I have the dogs." She pointed to an umbrella table in the corner of the grassy area in front of the hotel.

After Rick parked the car, all three of them sat down at a table in the shade of a cottonwood tree. Her two dogs, Rhonda and Stephanie, sat with their little pink tongues hanging out. Because of the warm weather, the little pooches panted in short breaths. Sheila was wearing jeans and a pink tee shirt. She tossed her blonde hair back, crossed her long legs, and started to talk about Jeff.

To Monica, it seemed she spouted like an erupting volcano. She evidently didn't believe one should speak only good of the dead. Sheila began her recital of Jeff's misbehavior. "That no-good jerk cheated on me and squandered his money on gambling and booze. He probably spent a lot of money on the local women he slept with, but he was tight as a tick with me. For my birthday, he gave me a popcorn popper, and he knew I didn't like popcorn. But he sure did. While he watched football, he would eat an entire bowl. Have you ever heard of a man who was that selfish? And did he ever remember Rhonda and Stephanie's birthday? Not once."

"Tell Detective Miller about his comment about the Mercedes," urged Monica.

"He said he was going to buy a Mercedes, a brand new Mercedes, with cash! He shut up when I asked how he could do that. But he had a secretive gleam in his eyes and chuckled. I knew something was 'up' which probably wasn't legal. He always had a get-rich scheme in mind that never worked."

"Very interesting."

"I want to go through his papers and see if I can figure out what he did or more important, if there is a pot of money somewhere. I'm his sole beneficiary, and I deserve something after giving him the best years of my life."

Rick shook his head and said, "We didn't find any large sum of money or any papers indicating he had bank accounts in Albuquerque or another city. Do you have any idea where he could have put important papers?"

"He didn't like banks because he said they were too snoopy. I think he rented a storage space. He did that before. Several years ago when we were late for the rent, he said he hid some rainy day money in a storage shed. He had a couple pieces of furniture in a small unit, and he put his money in the drawer of his grandmother's old-fashioned dresser. At that time we were still getting along, and he let me go with him to get the money. Weird , don't you think?" Sheila leaned back in her chair.

"We didn't find any storage key, just keys for his rental car, his house, and the hotel room," replied Rick. "Do you have any idea where he could hide a key?"

"Yes, sometimes he took a Bible with him. Not to read, of course, but one with a hollowed out space to put things. No one would open the cover of a Bible to see if it was really a book and not just a covered box." Sheila paused to put one of the dogs on her lap.

Rick's eyes perked up. "There was a Gideon's Bible in the bed side drawer in the murder room. We assumed it was part of the furnishings. Maybe it wasn't"

Sheila's eyes glistened. "Maybe it was his Bible. If I could find his money, I could buy a station wagon so the dogs would have more space when we travel. I could, also, buy some new clothes and a new washer and dryer." Monica watched as Sheila licked her lips in anticipation of the goodies she could have.

"That room is occupied right now since the hotel has a big Oz convention. I'll have to ask the manager about getting access to the Bible," added Rick.

"What's an Oz convention?" Monica asked as she put the other dog on her lap.

"People who like the Oz books get together for a convention. Since *Wicked* was so popular on Broadway, lots of people are reading *The Wizard of OZ* and the other Oz books. I'm lucky I got a room," said Sheila. "Tonight they have their big parade in which every one dresses like a character out of the book. I've seen about a dozen women dressed as Dorothy. One of them asked if she could rent out Stephanie as a substitute for Toto. I, of course, refused. The nerve of her!" While recalling that outrageous request, Sheila tightened her grip on Rhonda.

"I'd like to see the parade," said Monica.

"Let's go." Sheila became animated and picked up the two leashes. Each of the dogs hopped down from a lap and trotted over to her. In a slightly off-key voice Sheila started to sing, "We're off to see the Wizard, the wonderful Wizard of Oz."

Monica stood up, turned her head to Rick and whispered, "Although she is very hopeful of finding her pot of gold, I don't think she has any real information."

"I'd like to see that Bible because I doubt if any of my boys tried to flip through the pages," said Rick to Monica as they trailed behind the scampering dogs and the singing Sheila.

Once inside the hotel, they saw a cardboard yellow brick road which began at the entrance of the lobby and continued to the ballroom. The lobby was decorated like the Emerald City with all shades of green gauzy fabric draped over the potted palms and side tables. Green witches with pointy black hats, black robes, and funny broomsticks outnumbered the good witches who wore pink bouffant prom type dresses. Monica thought the show *Wicked* must have influenced this trend.

A couple scarecrows scratched their shoulders where bits of straw stuck out of their clothing. An aluminum costumed tin woodman held an oil can and spoke to a sweaty lion who had taken off his head and was fanning himself with his tail. Several Dorothys with pigtails and shiny red shoes looked covetously at Sheila's dogs as nice accompaniments to their costumes. Sheila seemed to have a maternal sense of this danger and picked up the dogs and tucked one under each arm.

Monica stood and gaped at this dazzling display while Rick went over to the desk to talk to the manager. A couple of children, or short adults dressed as Munchkins, hopped up and down as they tried to find someone in the crowd. More green witches got out of the elevator and blended into the coven.

A woman dressed in a pale lime gown with a crown on her head and carrying an un-Oz like clipboard shouted, "Everyone, let's take our places. Since I'm Ozma this year, I'll lead the parade. Then the Dorothys, the scarecrows, and the tin woodmen follow in that order." Lots of scrambling for position took place. Osma continued calling out the names of minor characters although it appeared to Monica the wicked witches of the west had taken over the convention, perhaps two or three covens of them.

One group of Oz inhabitants must have hit the bar beforehand since they were laughing, whooping it up, and gooseing each other with the broom sticks and having a wonderful time. Osma gave up on shushing them and led the parade with a smile and a glass of champagne. At the end of the parade marched the Wizard with his megaphone.

Rick returned and gave them the bad news. "The manager says I can't enter the room until it's unoccupied which won't be until Tuesday. I'd have to have a search warrant, and no judge is going to give me one without a really good reason. We'll just have to wait."

"I need to know now. I can't just wait around," moaned Sheila. "Who knows if that other jerk, John, will find it before I do. John's peace bit I'm sure is phony, but I don't know how." Sheila bit a corner of her lip in frustration.

"What do you know about John Spenser?" asked Rick.

"When Jeff read about him in the newspaper, he told me he wanted to get a job with him. He said it was a great opportunity. After Jeff started working for John, he was gone a lot. There were conventions, marches, and protests against war. John took in money at all these gatherings, but I don't know where the money went. I have my own opinion about that money, but no proof of anything that wasn't legit."

Monica nodded in agreement since she, too, suspected the money they collected wasn't going to Africa. Rick pulled out his cell phone, excused himself to make a call, and went to a quiet corner beside one of the funny gauzy trees. The Oz inhabitants marched through the lobby in rag tag fashion with lots of laughter and some yelps from people who were ahead of the witches wielding broomsticks.

Sheila looked at Monica and whispered, "I have an idea. Let's put on costumes and join the Oz group. We'll watch the talent show, and afterwards we'll find the people who are now staying in the room where Jeff died. We'll pretend we have a crisis and need to use a Bible. We'll tell them there wasn't a Bible in our room. Then the people staying in Jeff's room will offer their Bible, and we'll get it. That'll work, won't it?"

"How do we know who's in that room?"

"I have my ways," said Sheila confidently. "We need to look like part of the group so they'll feel a sense of comradeship. I have some clothes that could pass for a Dorothy costume. Do you think you could come up with something, too? We can use the dogs as our Totos."

Monica thought Miss Marple wouldn't miss an opportunity to do some detective work. Since the police could do nothing until Tuesday, she might get some evidence before they did. "It might be kind of fun. Sure, I'll help you out." She mentally went through her closet for a suitable costume. "I have a white blouse, an apron, and red sandals. Both of us could put our hair in pigtails, and with the dogs I think we could pass. I'll meet you back here in the lobby about 8:00 o'clock."

When Rick finished his call, Monica told him of their plan. He chuckled at first and then burst into loud laughter. "That's a crazy idea, but don't tell me any more. I don't want to know any details."

"Okay, this is a secret undercover operation. All details will be on a need-to-know basis, and you aren't on the list," said Monica to Rick. The two women exchanged meaningful looks. Monica's eyes sparkled as she anticipated their caper.

As Rick drove Monica home, he was still chuckling. "This is becoming a very unusual case with a particularly interesting person helping out."

Monica tried not to show how pleased she was with his comment; however, she felt her face get hot and hoped he didn't notice her rosy glow. They chatted briefly about the money Sheila thought Jeff had accumulated. They both decided the pot of money was probably a delusion Sheila fostered in her desire for a new vehicle.

When they arrived at Monica's apartment, Rick carried the cake and walked her to the door. As he handed it to her, she blurted out, "Would you like to come over for dinner tomorrow night, and we'll have butterscotch cake for dessert?"

Without a pause, he said, "I'd be delighted. What time shall I be here?"

"Come at 6:30. I know eating later is more fashionable, but I have a 7:30 class Monday morning." She almost felt faint after making such a bold move.

"Six thirty is great. See you then." He smiled as he waved good-bye.

"What a nice smile." thought Monica. But she didn't have time to think about his smile. She had to put on some sort of a Dorothy costume for tonight. Tomorrow she had a busy day since she had to plan a menu, clean her apartment a little, go to the grocery store, and review those notes on *Hamlet*. One thing at a time.

The sound of the opening door had triggered a dog response. Wagging her black tail with a tiny bit of white on the tip, Mitsey greeted her with a big sloppy kiss, and as usual she gave the dog a milk bone. The new cat, Bob, chomped Meow Mix from a bowl, and Marilyn used her paw to wash her face. Her little family appeared to be living in harmonious tranquility.

Monica opened her closet door and found an ironed, white blouse. Since pinafores were out of the question, she checked her skirts. She selected a gathered skirt with multicolored flowers and an old pair of red sandals. In her dresser drawer, she found two aprons: a plaid one with a picture of a barbecue grill, and a white one with Merry Christmas in green thread across the hem. She grabbed the Yuletide apron, dressed quickly, and plaited her hair into pig tails. Using her eyebrow pencil, she put a few freckles on her cheeks.

She petted each animal before she left on the Bible Caper. Mitsey went back to lie on the red sofa, while the two cats took off for the bed. Bob had adapted at an astonishing rate to his new home. Of course, Meow Mix and a down comforter helped with making the adjustment.

Back at the Barclay Towers, Monica went to the designated meeting place in the lobby and sat down to read the schedule of events for the convention which she had gotten from the reception desk. Starting at 9:00 tonight, the Wizard's Talent Show would take place in the ballroom, and tomorrow the Munchkin Brunchkin, the Flying Monkey Race, and the Broom and Ball competition would be held. None of these made any sense to her except the talent show which was due to start in 30 minutes.

The Oz inhabitants trickled into the lobby and brushed up on their skills. Four Munchkins sang in barbershop harmony "Down by the Old Brick Road," a tin man twirled a baton which barely missed the overhead light, a lion tuned a violin, and two scarecrows juggled funny looking black objects painted to resemble crows. While they tossed them back and forth, they made "caw"sounds.

Monica was so caught up in all the rehearsal activities she didn't see Sheila until she stood directly in front of her. Dressed in a white blouse and a black skirt, Sheila looked more like a waitress than a Dorothy.

"You take Stephanie," said Sheila as she handed over a leashed pooch to Monica. Excited by all the activity, Stephanie yipped a couple times and then strained at the leash to get to one of the fallen "crow" objects. Rhonda seemed more intrigued by two lions that were munching pretzels and swallowing beer. She pulled Sheila over a couple feet and managed to scarf down some pretzel crumbs.

A drunken Dorothy in a blue and white checked pinafore and red sparkly shoes raised an eyebrow at Monica and Sheila then said, "You two are the sorriest looking Dorothys I've seen." She shook her head at their disreputable costumes and moved on.

"People must take all of this very seriously," mused Monica. "Oh, by the way, do you know what a Flying Monkey Race is?"

"You buy a little four inch stuffed monkey with big paper wings and tie it to a balloon. At the signal, you let go of the string and blow the balloon and the paper wings toward the finish line. If you have too much down draft, the balloon with its monkey will hit the ground, and you're out of the race. The best way is to blow upward and horizontally at the same time. People bet on the monkeys and even train for the event." Sheila puckered her lips and blew into the air to show the proper technique.

"What do you mean 'train' for the event?"

"They take their monkeys home and practice blowing. Before the competition, the judges weigh each monkey to make sure someone hasn't removed any stuffing to make the monkey lighter and faster. You can only use your own breath, not any mechanized blower," explained Sheila who seemed to know all the details.

"I'd like to watch the race tomorrow, but I have a lot to do." Monica got a worried expression on her face while she mentally went through her list of things-to-do. But she quickly forgot these chores and thought of the coming adventure of the evening.

"Do you want to watch the Wizard's Talent Show? The people registered in the murdered man's room are competing. It's a husband and wife team from Iowa who plan to dance the Kansas Tornado Shuffle," said Sheila who was holding the leash tight while her dog strained to get going.

"Yes, let's watch them. I don't think they'd want to help us with our Bible emergency before the competition. By the way, what is our emergency?" Monica had to restrain her little Stephanie from climbing on a hotel sofa. It was hard to listen to Sheila and keep her eye on the pooch.

"I haven't figured out all the details yet, but you just got word your mother died or your brother died, and you're very depressed. You need to read the Bible for consolation, and our room doesn't have a Bible. How's that?" Sheila looked very proud of her story line.

Monica nodded. "It sounds okay to me. I'll try to look grief stricken when you give me the sign." The Bible Caper was ready to go.

8

When Monica and Sheila entered the ballroom, the Oz inhabitants were milling around, drinking beer or whiskey, and telling jokes. The two dogs strained at their leashes as they looked and sniffed at shoes, potted palms, and sofas. A tipsy Munchkin tripped over Stephanie who gave out a little yelp of pain. Monica bent down, touched the little head, and crooned a soothing sound to make her feel better.

The two women found seats, picked up the dogs, put them in their laps, and settled in for the talent show. The Wizard, a short man with a tall hat, went to center stage and welcomed the convention goers. As everyone clapped loudly, Stephanie and Rhonda got in the spirit of the occasion and howled. Monica looked around, but no one seemed to care the dogs were barking.

A minute later Stephanie spotted another Toto impersonator, jumped off Monica's lap, and took off to visit the new dog. Little Rhonda made a dash for freedom, too, and now both dogs were dodging in and out of chair legs and dragging leashes that oddly enough had not gotten caught on any feet, purses, or objects.

Both Monica and Sheila made desperate grabs for leashes but failed. Since they were in the middle of the row, they tried to make themselves thin and not stumble over people's feet while saying, "Excuse me, I'm sorry, excuse me." Because the atmosphere was so chaotic, Monica felt the dogs could chase each other around the room, and no one would even notice.

Meanwhile the owner of another impersonator Toto said, "Where are your mommies?" to the errant dogs. The Oz citizens near the pooches laughed good heartedly. Sheila reached the dogs first and picked one up in each hand. They licked her in the face and showed no sign of guilt for bad behavior.

"I'm so sorry," murmured Sheila.

"They're adorable," replied the lady. "My little one is overly excited, too." Monica looked down and observed her dog lying down with his head on his paws.

Returning to their seats, Monica and Sheila repeated their earlier trip with, "Sorry again, excuse me, so sorry."

With dogs in laps and tight grips on collars, they both looked at the stage. The Munchkin Quartet sang "Down by the Old Brick Road" while several members of the audience hummed along. When they finished, everyone gave them a standing ovation. As the evening entertainment continued, the audience gave every act a standing ovation. A standing audience made it easy for some of the members to slip away to refill their empty glasses.

Finally, the Wizard announced the Kansas Tornado Shuffle team. Auntie Em in a gingham blue and white dress with a big, white apron and a sun bonnet walked on the stage and made a tiny bow. She curled her index finger and wiggled it in the universal gesture of "come here." Her husband in bib overalls shuffled over to her. The music for "Tea for Two" began, and they both put out the right foot, tapped it, shuffled the left, and moved back and forth in time with the three beat music. Auntie Em twirled around several times while her husband held her hand high over her head. Neither one looked at the audience.

After several minutes, a stage hand turned on a large fan and switched it on high which imitated a wind storm. The couple swayed back and forth, made circles on the stage while flaying their arms, and opened their mouths in the shape of an O. The fan blew Auntie Em's sun bonnet off and rustled her skirt. With a kerplunk, they both fell on the floor. Again a standing ovation while the couple, flushed with success, bowed.

"Do you think we should approach them now?" asked Monica.

"No, not yet. They won't want to leave the area until the winner is announced. I've talked to them already in passing, and they hope to win. Their act was corny, but so are most of them. So who knows? The three judges are already smashed."

An hour later after seven or eight more acts, the Wizard announced the soprano lion who sang "Memories" while dressed in a fur bikini was the winner. When she came on stage and bowed, her top almost fell off. The male members of the audience kept clapping. Monica decided they hoped she might bow even deeper the next time. When she left the stage with her top still holding fast, Monica noted the disappointed droop in the men's expressions.

"Now, " said Sheila, "let's park in the lobby. You pretend you hear your cell phone ring, pick it up, and look stricken. We have to make this look good in case there are witnesses. Then we'll go to our room, pretend we're looking for a Bible, search out the nice couple who have the room next to us, ask them for the Bible, and we're home free."

Monica was in awe of how well Sheila had organized this caper. Off hand, she couldn't think of any snags, but one never knew. After they sat down in the lobby, Monica went into her charade. She picked up her phone on its imaginary ring, pretended to listen, scrunched up her eyes, and sniffled. "I just got word my brother had a car accident and is in the hospital! I need a Bible bad."

"Oh, that's terrible, honey. Let's go up to our room and hope some kind Gideon has put a Bible in the night side table." Sheila's face drooped, although Monica couldn't see anyone looking or listening. "Such an awful thing to happen in the middle of our convention!"

Both women stood up, put the dogs on the floor, held kleenex to their eyes, and headed for the elevators. Once in the elevator by themselves, Monica questioned the charade, "Why do we have to actually go to the room? I don't think anyone is watching."

"Later, the police might ask for witnesses," said Sheila. "We have to cover all traces."

Monica began to wonder if Sheila had done something like this before. If Leslie had been her companion, they probably would have just asked the couple for the Bible without any of this play acting.

Once the elevator door opened on their floor, Sheila continued with her act. "That's just terrible. We'll see if there's a Bible in our room." After they entered, Sheila found the Gideon Bible in the bed side table and put it under the mattress. "Just in case someone checks our room. We should wait about five minutes to show we're searching."

"I really don't think all this is necessary," murmured Monica. She let Stephanie down on the floor to romp; the dog might as well enjoy the time. Sheila did likewise. The two dogs chased each other under the table and sniffed around. "Maybe they have to go," suggested Monica. "It would be awkward to have to take them outside just when we're in the middle of our desperate need for a Bible."

"They were out for a walk before you came. They're just sniffing." Sheila looked at her watch. "Maybe a couple minutes more."

Monica sighed. She thought all of this play acting was crazy. She wondered if Sheila had done impromptu acting in college or been involved in sting operations. "Sheila, are you an actress?"

"I've done a few shows in summer stock and once a show in Chicago, but nothing on film," she said in a modest voice. "I hope to do television, but it's hard. There are so many young hopefuls in the business."

"I've heard it's not easy to get that break. By the way, where did you meet Jeff?"

"I met him at a cast party when I did the show in Chicago. He praised my work in the play and told me I was the most beautiful women he had ever seen. I married the jerk the next year. He and Larry opened a used car business, but they needed more money and started taking bets for everything. Jeff lost money, but Larry picked the good ponies, the good football teams, the good whatever teams. Later, Jeff heard about John and went out to meet him. It wasn't long before he was part of John's team."

"Why did he want to work for John Spenser and the peace movement?"

"He just said it was a good opportunity. At that time I was cast as one of the witches in *Macbeth,* and I was too busy rehearsing to ask many questions. By the way, Jeff never supported me in my career. In fact he made snide comments. He said the director knew what he was doing when he cast me as a witch. What a jerk."

By this time, Sheila decided they could leave the room and look for the Kansas-Tornado-Shuffle couple. Sheila snapped on the leashes for the dogs, and they walked out. Even though there wasn't a soul in sight in the hallway, Sheila held a kleenex to her eyes and indicated Monica should do the same. Monica almost giggled as she dabbed at her dry eyes.

Once they were in the lobby, they searched for their prey. Lots of noise and music drifted out from the bar which seemed a natural place for the revelers. Sheila spotted Larry at a table near the front of the bar. "He's probably taking bets on the Flying Monkey Contest. Monkey number 10 has won for the past three years so he's the favorite."

"How do you know Monkey number 10 is a favorite?" asked Monica breaking her pathetic facial appearance as she looked at her friend in a perplexed way.

"I get around. We'll talk later. Keep in character!"

Monica tried to look forlorn as she scanned the crowd. The sharp-eyed Sheila pounced on the couple who were sitting on a couch while sipping beer. "I hate to bother you, but my friend just heard her brother was involved in a terrible accident. She needs help from the Lord. We don't have a Bible in our room. Could we possibly use yours?" pleaded Sheila.

Monica pretended extreme distress. "I'm so worried about my brother."

Auntie Em jumped up and said, "Of course, dear, you need the Good Book. Let's go up right now and get it." Her husband didn't move a muscle. He obviously was content to let his wife do all the good Samaritan stuff while he sipped his beer.

Since Monica didn't know what to say, she just kept sniffling into her kleenex. Sheila kept chatting. "It's terrible they let men drive when they're drunk. What's this country coming to? They allow men to get behind the wheel after drinking all night at some sleazy bar while their children probably need the money for milk."

Auntie Em replied, "It's a crying shame. We've got to put those drunks in jail." She kept shaking her head. She put her arm around Monica and said, "Don't you worry, I'll get you a Bible, dearie." When they entered her room, she opened the drawer on the bedside table and took out the Bible. The dogs followed along without being distracted.

"I'll find a verse from the Good Book that should help you, " said Auntie Em.

"Noooo, that won't be necessary. I'll find one," purred Sheila as she reached for the book.

But Auntie Em had already started to leaf through the New Testament. Suddenly she squealed, "Someone has blasphemed! Someone cut the Good Book and took out the middle of the pages. Why? This person is going straight to Hell! Look, just look, at what's been done."

Sheila didn't miss a beat. "How awful! Let me see. There's a key tucked in that little space. I'll just remove it and take it and the book down to the reception desk. They'll know what to do about it."

Impressed by Sheila's fast thinking, Monica tried to go back into her role instead of gawking. "Yes, that's terrible. We should definitely take it to the hotel people."

Holding the book and key in one hand and the leash in another, Sheila bolted for the door. Auntie Em still in a daze said, "In all my born days, I've never seen anything like that. Such blasphemy! I've got to tell my husband." All three quickly left the room.

Auntie Em kept repeating, "What a terrible thing. Who could have done such a thing to the Good Book?" They charged down the hallway and went into the elevator. Auntie Em didn't stop talking until they left the elevator and walked into the lobby. The distressed woman headed for her husband while Sheila and Monica walked over to the reception desk.

The clerk looked up and asked, "Could I help you?"

Sheila asked, "What time does the Munchkin Brunchkin start?" Monica was impressed with Sheila's skill in handling the situation. If Auntie Em looked over at the desk, she would think Monica was telling the clerk about the damaged Bible.

"Tomorrow morning at 10:00 o'clock in the ballroom."

"Thank you," said Sheila while giving the clerk a smile. She put the book and key into her purse, turned her head to Monica, and whispered, "Let's get out of here."

They walked out into the warm night air with the dogs eagerly following them. Once they spotted a shrub, the dogs sniffed contentedly at some message left by other canines while the two women talked. Thrilled by the success of their caper, Monica could hardly contain her delight. "You were right. Can you tell what storage company he used?"

Sheila's eyes glittered as she clutched the key. "There isn't any name on the key so I'll have to try each storage company. Too bad they close up at night, or I'd start right now. I just have a feeling I'll find some money. Tomorrow I'll get an early start although I hate to miss the Munchkin Brunchkin."

Monica waited to be invited on the search, but Sheila didn't ask her. Monica consoled herself by thinking of all the things she needed to do tomorrow. Especially important was the dinner for Rick. As she thought about him, she wondered if Sheila intended to inform the detective about the key in the Bible. "Do you plan to tell Detective Miller about your find?"

"Of course, I'll tell him. Monica, you shouldn't say anything to anybody until I go to the police. I don't know what the key opens. It might not be a lock on a storage unit. It could just be a diary or something."

"How's it going?" came a voice from behind. Monica turned her head and saw Larry ambling towards them with his hands in his pockets. "Hey, you girls look real nice. You look like you're part of the gang. I've been in the bar and tossing back a few with some of the guys. Want to take some action on the Flying Monkey Race?"

Sheila shook her head. "Larry, you know I don't gamble. I've seen Jeff take too many losses."

"You think he hid some money?" Larry abruptly asked Sheila.

Monica wondered if Sheila would tell him her idea about the storage unit, but she just shrugged her shoulders and said, "I don't know. The jerk owes me a lot for all those years I stayed with him."

"He owes me, too, for a little business deal we had."

"If there is money, it's mine according to his will. I'll, of course, pay any bills. Larry, do you have any paper that shows Jeff owed you money?"

"Yeah, I got an IOU."

Monica didn't know what game they were playing, but the two of them looked at each other warily. Sheila broke the silence by taking the leash from Monica, tugging the two dogs towards the hotel door, and saying over her shoulder, "See you later."

Monica said, "Good night," to both of them and headed for her car. She wondered what the result of the Bible Caper would be, but she was tired and wanted to be home with her animals.

9

Monica scurried around her apartment cleaning the bathroom, setting the table in her little dining area, and picking up the stray books, glasses, and dirty plates in her living room. Bob, as the new cat, didn't show much initiative about examining his surroundings, but Marilyn, as the established know-it-all cat followed Monica all morning and meowed for treats.

Monica firmly believed in fairness so when she gave a treat to the begging Marilyn, she hunted down Bob and gave him a treat, too. Mitsey, who didn't want any other animal to get privileged treatment, showed up for her dog cookie. Monica didn't mind all these accommodations for her little family because she liked to feed them.

The telephone rang just as she was rinsing off the dog saliva from her hand. "Hi, this is Rick. Would you like to go to a rather unusual event called the Flying Monkey Race before our dinner date?"

Monica chuckled, "Yes, Sheila told me about it last night, and it sounds fun and crazy. Larry is even taking bets on it."

" I thought you'd like to see it. I'll pick you up in an hour."

During that hour, Monica washed the lettuce, tomatoes, and spinach for the salad, took the fish out of the freezer, located the bottle of a special sauce for the salmon, and got out the box of Minute Rice. After setting the table with her new blue flowered place mats, her dinner prep was done.

Rick showed up exactly on time. When she opened the door, he smiled at her and complimented her outfit, a blue sweater with a white lace camisole. He spoke to Mitsey and patted her head. In return, Mitsey wagged her tail with pleasure. Monica thought Rick was definitely making points.

When they arrived at the hotel, they noticed part of the parking lot was roped off. Several men sat at the judging tables and checked off names. At another table, the little stuffed monkeys with long red paper wings were weighed. Each entry had a number on the left wing. A large sign read, "Any contestant weighing less than one ounce will be disqualified."

Sheila said, "Sometimes the monkey owners took stuffing out to make their entries lighter. Larry told me all about the ways the owners could cheat."

An official of the contest placed each monkey tied to a balloon on a raised board about five feet off the ground. Straight ahead about twenty feet away a chalk mark indicated the finish line. The officials even had a camera set up to take a picture if two entries came in close. At the ringing of a bell, each man with his hands clasped behind him, started to blow.

The tiny animals took off on their twenty yard course. A gentle breeze blew enough to pitch a couple monkeys off course. Their owners frantically tried to correct the misdirection by blowing at an angle. A few monkeys crashed after this natural catastrophe. Monica could tell this contest required a certain skill.

"The favorite is Number 10," said Sheila, "but he isn't looking good." They watched as Number 10's wing dipped to the right at a rapid pace. His owner contorted his head and blew from below. The wing lifted; Number 10 could still win.

Photographers were busy with their cameras since these tiny flying monkeys made quite an unusual show. The breeze moved the little tails which looked like little wagging signs of happiness at flying into the wild blue yonder. Yells of "Go, Go, Baby!" could be heard coming from the sidelines.

A concession man came through with popcorn and hot dogs and another with cokes which created a ball park festive air. However, a few minutes later, a lady with a hand fan caused a small dustup. Even though she hadn't caused one little wave, she was asked to leave. Mechanical bursts of air were strictly forbidden.

A couple more monkeys crashed and were carried off the field. Number 10's owner had turned red in the face, but he kept up the air flow. He seemed to anticipate the ups and downs of his animal and kept gyrating his body to get the best angle to blow which not only kept the monkey afloat but progressed it forward. Monica heard someone say, "He's a real pro."

Number 10 passed the finish line way ahead of the others. Loud clapping burst out, and the judge brought over a small flowered garland which he placed on the monkey's shoulders. Grinning from ear to ear, the owner bowed while holding his charge in the palm of his hand.

A lady next to Monica said, "He practices his blowing technique all year long." After the excitement ended, the group disbursed and headed for the hotel.

Smiling at the incongruity of taking this cute event seriously, Monica said to Rick, "That lady said he trained for a year. Can you believe it? His neighbors must have questioned his sanity."

Rick shook his head back and forth. "I've never seen anything like it in my life. By the way, I noticed a flurry of activity at Larry's table. I wonder if he made a few bucks off this little, and I do mean little, race."

Monica looked across the parking lot and saw Larry counting some bills. John, seated next to him, glumly sipped a drink. Dressed in white shorts and a tight blue tee shirt, Jessica sat next to John and played with the straw in her coke. She leaned over and whispered in his ear before walking toward the hotel with her perky pony tail bouncing as she sashayed across the parking lot. As soon as she was out of sight, John slipped some money to Larry. Monica guessed I'll-never-er-gamble-again John had just lost a bet.

When John looked up from his drink, he waved at Monica and Rick and gestured for them to come over to his table. Rick pulled over a couple extra chairs, and the newcomers sat down. "How's it going, Rick? Found the killer yet?" asked John.

"We're making a few inquiries. Nothing definite."

"You got zilch!" interpreted Larry who scratched his chin and jiggled his foot while he spoke.

Rick, however, didn't answer the taunt. He shrugged his shoulders and changed the subject. He looked at John and inquired, "Do you have any future plans?"

"We have a convention in Atlanta in two weeks, but we can't find the hotel or airline reservations. Jeff made all the arrangements on the staff computer. Somebody at the police station has his laptop which I need right now. Do you know when I can get it? "

Rick nodded and answered, "The lab boys should be through with it. I'll talk to them and see if you can pick it up on Monday."

"Thanks, I appreciate it."

"No problem," replied Rick as he studied each face of the group seated around the table. "We try to return property as soon as we can."

"I'll tell Randy to pick up the laptop so I can find out what reservations he made. But since I'll be here for awhile, I made a few plans. Randy set up a speaking engagement with the preacher of a church here in Albuquerque. It's the Church of the Sun and Moon, and the guy's name is Star B. Stephens. He wants me to speak to his congregation tomorrow night." John gave his knuckles a couple cracks as he talked.

"Isn't that the church Elizabeth Harkenstone sponsors?" asked Monica as she turned to Rick.

"Yes, that's the one. She's a life long resident here in Albuquerque," Rick said as he crossed his legs and leaned back in his chair.

"Who's Elizabeth Harkenwhatever?" asked John.

Monica chimed in, "I know a lot about her. She's a very wealthy eccentric who owns many commercial buildings, acres of land, and a fat portfolio of stock. Her father made a fortune in oil. She's quite a philanthropist, but a little dotty. She gives heavily to the Church of the Sun and Moon and believes that its founder, Star B. Stephens, is a miracle worker. By the way, the B. in his name stands for Burst."

"Really, how interesting," mused John.

At that point, Jessica returned and addressed Monica and Rick. "It's so nice to see you both again. Wasn't that a charming race? Those sweet little monkeys up in the air like that. They looked so precious. But can you believe people were making bets? I'm so glad John has stopped gambling. It's a bad, bad habit." While babbling, she fluffed up her pony tail and angled her face toward John.

Monica stole a quick look at John, but she saw no pink glow of embarrassment on his face. He just grinned, reached out, and patted Jessica's hand. She responded by giving him her usual adoring look.

Randy now approached the table at a jaunty clip. When she arrived at the table, Rick pushed out a chair for her since John made no effort to even acknowledge her entrance. Randy slapped down her notebook on the table and announced, "I've just spoken with Star. Everything is set for your speaking engagement at the

Church of the Sun and Moon." John nodded, but kept looking into Jessica's worshipful eyes. Randy inhaled deeply, shot him a baleful glance, and bit her lip. "I said," she snapped, "everything is set with the church!" The volume and the narrowed, hate filled eyes sent a message which Monica believed everyone at the table got.

"Fine," he answered. "Thanks." His voice was calm, but Monica caught a tone of contempt.

"I'm going to go with John when he speaks tomorrow night at the church," said Jessica with a triumphant ring to her voice. "Thank you, Randy, for making the arrangements."

Monica could tell Randy didn't take this putdown well. Her eyes hurled sharp daggers at perky Miss Pony Tail and at John who was smiling at his attractive disciple. Randy demanded, "John, we need to talk."

"Later," he said in a low voice.

Randy huffed, turned on her heel, and strode off in the direction of the hotel.

"I don't know what got into her. She acts like she owns me," said John to the group sitting at the table. "But let's change the subject. What is this Ball and Broomstick game?"

Rick explained, "It's sort of like golf with balls and broomsticks. Each player is supposed to hit the ball as far as he can. The judges have markers on the parking lot to indicate how many yards the ball went. Each player has five shots. The winner, of course, is the player who can hit the ball the farthest. By the way, the brooms have to be regulation straw ones they sell at the convention otherwise someone could use a really stiff bristled one and have a distinct advantage."

"I'm not taking any action on those games. Those guys get gassed and sometimes even miss the ball," explained Larry who fidgeted with his fingers on the table.

"Do both men and women witches play ?" asked Monica who wanted to be sure there was no gender bias."

"Yes, but, in general, more men go out for the game," said Rick. "Sometimes the game gets a little violent. If a player hits another player with his broom, he's out." Rick made a gesture with his thumb to indicate what happens to an unruly participant.

A gaggle of green witches with their pointy black hats started to gather as the judges were marking the parking lot with chalk to indicate the yardage. Monica couldn't figure out who was male and who was female

Some of the witches carried their brooms over their shoulders like guns while others rode them and galloped around like kids. A few who had been dragging their brooms suddenly got lively and joined in the merry making by pretending to have a duel with swords as they thrust and parried their brooms. So far, no one got goosed.

A tall witch with two dogs on leashes tapped Monica on the shoulder. "Would you watch Rhonda and Stephanie while I take a shot at the prize?"

Monica, of course, recognized the dogs, but had to peer intently at the face with the black wig and big hat. "Of course."

"Sheila, dear, I should have recognized you right away since you look like the person Jeff always said he was married to," joked John.

"Very funny," said Sheila in a clipped, low voice.

"Maybe he said it with a 'B' sound instead," bantered John, "but seriously, do you have any ideas about the whereabouts of Jeff's mythical pot of gold?"

"I haven't a clue," answered Sheila who made a quick glance over at Monica who fluffed her short brown hair and tried to look like a person who wasn't going to spill the beans.

"Please, let me know since I have a bill for the cremation," added John.

"Of course, John, it was so nice seeing you again," said Sheila whose voice was dripping with sarcasm. She almost tripped over her broom as she left the table to join the coven at the lineup.

Stephanie and Rhonda yipped and tugged at their leashes when Sheila left. Monica bent down and petted each little head and made soothing noises, "She'll be back soon."

While she was still bent over fussing with the little dogs, she heard John whisper to Larry, "I bet Sheila knows more than she's telling about Jeff's hidden money. I'm going to keep close tabs on her."

Jessica, who had been sitting quietly, decided to talk to the furry creatures. She crooned, "What sweet doggies." Then she moved so she could stroke their silky hair. With the attention, both dogs lost interest in making a break for it and basked in the soft female sounds.

At the sound of a trumpet, the first contestant approached the line, swung his broom, and sent the ball to the 10 yard line. The rest of the coven didn't form a nice straight line behind the starting position but instead milled about while brandishing their broomsticks all over the place. One took a practice swing and knocked over a fellow contestant's hat which caused a minor tiff but no blows were exchanged.

Monica couldn't recognize Sheila in the mass of black robes, but she bet if she let go of the leashes, the dogs would easily find her. These costumes certainly made it easy for someone to hide his or her identity.

This contest didn't have the appeal of the flying monkey affair so Monica let her eyes run over the crowd. It wasn't long before Sheila came to retrieve her dogs. She took the leashes and sat down at the crowded table

John leaned over to talk to Sheila, " I'm going to speak tomorrow night at the Church of the Sun and Moon. Jessica and I plan to have a little supper afterwards. Would you like to go? I promise I won't make any more bad jokes."

Sheila thought for a moment. "I'll go if Monica will go with me. How about it?"

"Sure, I'll go. It should be interesting. I've heard Star has gotten quite a following in Santa Fe, and some of the people who believe in crystals are switching to worshiping the sun and the moon."

Monica wondered if John was "making nice" to Sheila so he could get more information out of her. Both John and Sheila seemed to have a lightly concealed hostile relationship. She knew Sheila thought John was a sham and a scoundrel, but she wasn't sure why John didn't like Sheila. The evening probably would give her more insight into their lives, and perhaps into the life of Jeff. Was there really a pot of hidden money?

While spending the evening together, she would warn Sheila about John and his interest in keeping tabs on her. Tonight, she had a lot to tell Rick about the adventures of last night. After months of teaching and grading papers, she now had a very interesting life outside of school.

10

On Monday night, Monica drove to the Barclay Towers to pick up Sheila. Monica really would have preferred Leslie's company, but the invitation hadn't included another guest. The two women would meet up with John and his date, Jessica, at the Church of the Sun and Moon where he would give his lecture.

Feeling well-dressed in her new navy blue suit, Monica walked into the lobby of the hotel. Sheila was sitting on a sofa waiting for her.

"What did you do with the dogs?" Monica asked.

"I couldn't take them to the church so I asked John if they could stay in his suite. He has a bedroom and another room he uses as an office so they'll have more room to run around. My bedroom is so tiny."

"Sounds good for the dogs," Monica said. "And, by the way, have you checked the storage companies to see if Jeff hoarded some money there?"

"Well, a little bit, but there are many, many storage companies so it's going to take a long time," replied Sheila. "You know I'm going to this wacky church in order to keep tabs on John."

"He told me he had to keep tabs on you," giggled Monica. "You two must have an interesting relationship."

"We know each other. I've watched him operate since he was in the used car business with Larry. He might be up to something. If he finds Jeff's money, he sure isn't going to tell me. I could ask Randy since I think that she's *had it* with John. Randy has been his girlfriend for years, and she's put up with a lot. But this Jessica thing is going farther than his usual one-night-stands with local girls."

"Do you think Randy will come tonight?" asked Monica as they walked out.

"Probably, she set up the speaking engagement, and I know she'll have her claws out for sweet, innocent Miss Pony Tail."

The two women drove in silence for awhile until they saw the church. The two-story, white office building sat amidst several large cottonwood trees. On a pole in the front, a large golden globe light dominated the landscape. Yellow plastic covered wires were stuck to the globe in order to give the appearance of sun beams. Monica wondered if they used Gorilla glue to fasten wires to glass. On another pole, a white globe shot out beams made from white plastic covered wires.

A chubby man wearing a blue velvet robe with satin sun, moon, and stars prominently displayed on the front walked out to greet them. "Welcome to the Church of the Sun and Moon. May the sun warm your spirit and may the moon comfort your dreams." He was smiling, and his round face and rounder tummy made him look like the Pillsbury Dough Boy.

"Thank you," murmured Monica. She hadn't expected a welcome from the chief honcho. His robe was a little over the top, but since he came from Santa Fe, she expected restrained eccentricity.

"Please follow me. John and his other guest are already here. I'm Star Stephens, your galaxy leader." He opened the door which lead into a lobby area of the office building. The walls had been decorated with various renditions of the universe from different angles. Star kept walking while explaining the various areas of his church.

"In our house of worship, we have rooms named after the planets. The biggest room, of course, is the Sun Room where we'll gather tonight. I'll tell you both just a few things about our church because you must be curious." Star seemed eager to show off his church. Although the office building had been renovated, the structure remained the same, a long hallway with doors on each side.

Monica and Sheila followed him as he pointed out Saturn's Salad Bar on the left, Pluto's Coffee Bar on the right, and Mercury's Gift Shop straight ahead. They could smell pizza coming from Pallas's Pizza Parlor just past the Saturn's Salad Bar. In each area people were either eating or chatting. "All of these little shops are part of our church and bring in good revenue," he explained. When they came to Jupiter's Boutique, Star stopped and gestured for them to enter.

He introduced them to Melody, the owner and designer of the clothing. She smiled sweetly. "I originated the Rapture line of clothing. It's a niche that needed to be filled. So I worked hard on my designs because I believe people want to look their best on the

Big Day. I have robes in heavenly white, celestial blue, and paradise green. All the robes are embroidered in gold thread. If you wish, I can add a monogram, for an extra price, of course."

Star smiled and added, "This Rapture line is going like a house afire. We just can't keep enough stock on hand. We don't know for sure when the Rapture is coming, but as Melody says, no one wants to look shoddy on their first day Up There. You've got to be prepared. I suggest each person should have several robes on hand just in case of spills. Red wine stains are so hard to get out."

"Maybe the just serve white wine Up There," said Monica. After she spoke, she thought she might have sounded a little sarcastic. Star didn't give her a sharp look, so she hoped he wasn't offended.

Sheila, on the other hand, had picked up a hanger with a celestial blue robe with a golden belt and was holding it in front of her as she looked in a full length mirror. "How much is this one?"she inquired.

Melody checked the tag. "Five hundred dollars. Notice the gold inlay on the belt and on the neckline. This is our most popular number. We have another model with fuller sleeves if you want a more flowing look. It costs a little more, but cost should not be a concern when you're buying something this important. We also have a style with a long sweeping train. You need to turn carefully so you don't step on the satin. That costs one thousand dollars, but it is truly beautiful."

Monica didn't want to offend Melody, but she was curious so she spoke out, "Is it all right to wear these robes on other occasions? Since there might be quite a wait for the, ahhhh Rapture, perhaps people might wear them before?"

Melody sniffed with displeasure. "We can't control when people wear Rapture clothes, but we definitely hope they don't wear them for earthly occasions. They should want their garment fresh and clean for the Big Day."

Star's three or four chins nodded in agreement. "But as I've said before, we encourage members of our flock or anyone else, of course, to buy several robes. It's good to have an extra on hand. Don't you just love the styles? I have four myself."

Monica felt she should say something nice. "All the models are lovely."

Melody and Star beamed with pleasure. Sheila by now had taken out several robes and held them in front of her while she looked in the mirror.

Melody said, "I think the heavenly white with the seed pearls goes beautifully with your complexion. Would you like to try it on?"

"I'll think it over," replied Sheila which was the standard female way of saying that she's not interested.

Melody cautioned, "Don't wait too long. You never know when the Rapture is coming. I always tell my customers it's better to be prepared than sorry later on."

Monica now felt a little naughty, but she couldn't resist asking, "What if you're not going Up There, but

Down There?" She pointed with her finger at the floor. "Do you sell any fiery red numbers?"

"No!" said Melody emphatically. "They can wear their tattered jeans, for all I care."

Star, however, seemed to be musing over the proposition. "I hadn't thought of that before. Melody, we should perhaps give that idea a think before we dismiss it."

Everyone paused, and Monica thought perhaps Melody was contemplating this new line of appropriate clothing for Down There. Monica controlled her giggles but didn't dare look at Sheila for fear they might erupt. Star, by now, had decided to resume his tour, and they all walked out of the shop.

"Melody is such as asset to our church, and she's just cute as a button," chirped Star. He continued leading the way, "Our Sun Room is upstairs."

As they climbed the stairs, Monica asked Star, "Could you explain your theology?"

"We believe the sun is the most important thing in the universe. We couldn't grow a darn thing without the sun. Just think, no crops, no tomatoes, no trees, no oranges. We also need the sun for light. How would you like to stumble around with a flashlight all the time? And what about a tan? Sun bathing would be non-existent. You'd have to buy your tan from one of those bottles and smear it on. I tried that once, and it was yucko."

"Yes, we really do need the sun," said Monica, "but what about the moon?"

"The moon is important, too. It controls the tides. The oceans's sloshing back and forth is very relaxing. I just love to go to California, get a hotel by the beach, and listen to that whooshing sound of the water. In the morning I go looking for shells the tide brought in. We need the moon. Because of its beauty, it inspires songs. Stars are okay, but they just don't have as much glamour."

With a straight face, Monica replied, "I love songs about love in the moon light."

"I don't want to dis the stars. They're pretty, and gosh, my name is Star Burst so I really do like stars. But you have to admire old man moon who changes all the time. I like the crescent moon the best although the full moon can't be beat."

"I don't think anyone could argue with your theology," stated Monica. In her inner thoughts, she was musing how could anyone take this guy seriously. He had such a cherubic face and lots of childish enthusiasm which wasn't the usual case for religious swindlers. Evidently people had given him money, or he wouldn't have this building. Unless, of course, his rich father had left him millions.

Sheila kept showing interest in the murals as they climbed the stairs. She didn't indicate with eye rolls or circular hand motions against the head that Star didn't fit into the ordinary sane world. She merely nodded her head a lot as if she thought he was normal with normal ideas. A good actress. Monica hoped her performance was convincing, too.

On entering the Sun Room, Monica stopped in her tracks to take it all in. The room was painted yellow with a huge gold plated sun on one wall. The lights shone down on rows of gold enameled chairs with a special spot light on a satin covered throne that faced the others. Wooden gold poles stuck out of the back of the chair making a curve over the top. To Monica, it looked like a picket fence had been nailed to the chair to form sun beams. She wondered if he had been inspired by renditions of Our Lady of Guadalupe. Since the chair was padded and had a couple loose pillows, it appeared to be rather comfortable in a bizarre way.

Monica spotted John and Jessica sitting together in the back row. Star indicated that Monica and Sheila should sit next to his other guests.

"This is so great to have such a celebrity here tonight. And, of course, you girls too." Star's smile showed off his dimples.

John smoothly replied, "It is an honor for me to visit your church and to have an opportunity to speak to your congregation about the great need for peace." Wearing a navy suit with a white shirt and stripped tie, John looked very conventional. Jessica, attired in a white tailored blouse with black skirt, fit in with main stream America and not this alternative religious service.

"Most of the Sun and Moon worshipers like to eat a bite in the cafes downstairs, but they'll be here soon. Mrs. Harkenstone, our Moon Goddess, spends her afternoons in the Moon Room and will join us later."

"Do you have a service once a week?" asked Monica.

"Usually we do unless there's a special occasion. Tomorrow night we're all going to the opera in Santa Fe. They're doing *The Magic Flute* by Mozart. We love the scenes with the Queen of the Night. It's so appropriate with our theme. Mrs. Harkenstone, who loves opera, graciously buys all our tickets," chirped Star.

At that point, an old lady with tightly permed gray hair entered. She was short and chubby, much like Star, sort of a Tweedledum and Tweedledee couple. The Moon Goddess wore a black satin gown with a huge moon made of pearls on the front panel. As she slipped into the room, she held out both her hands to John and then to the rest of the party.

"My dears, how lovely to have you come to our sacred place. I welcome you in the name of the Moon and, of course, the Sun. These two celestial bodies are the most important in the world. How could we live without the Sun and the Moon? We must worship them and let them know how much we love them."

Mrs. Harkenstone, the Moon Goddess, gave Star, the Sun God, a big hug. Then she lifted his arm high in the air. Hands clasped with outstretched arms, the two struck a triumphant pose. The Moon Goddess shouted out in a strident voice, "We two rule the entire world!" No one laughed. This proclamation by an old lady and a middle-aged man, both overweight and wearing Halloween costumes, didn't look like a danger to the free world.

After a few moments, Star took his seat on the golden throne while the Moon Goddess sat in the back on the regular chairs for the congregation. "We take turns," she whispered. "Our next meeting will be in the Moon Room."

Monica bet there was another throne in the Moon Room, just as fancy. The Moon Goddess wouldn't like to play second fiddle.

The room began to fill with the members of the congregation. Some of them were wearing tie-dye clothes from the old hippie era, while others wore fashionable jeans with holes in them. They quieted down after they were seated, and Star stood and made a round circle with his finger in the air in front of his chest. Everyone did the same thing. Then Star flung out his arms and shouted, "I love you, Sun."

All the Sun Rays chanted, "I love you, Sun."

"Instead of our regular worship tonight, we have a celebrity with us who wants to share his message with you," announced Star. "Let's give John Spenser our special sunshine welcome."

The group, still standing, said in chorus, "We, Sun Rays, welcome you into the sphere of light." John took that as a cue and stood up and walked slowly to the front of the room. Evidently he had decided his usual energetic pace and leap didn't fit this situation.

"Thank you, very much. I'm very happy to meet with you all tonight. My message is peace. The Sun and Moon want peace in their world. The Sun and Moon want to look over the world and see everyone in harmony."

He shaped his old speech to dovetail into this church's mold with alacrity and skill. He said, "The Sun and the Moon don't want war and especially don't want little babies burned up in the terrible conflicts." His eyes frequently looked at the Moon Goddess. When he mentioned the death of children, he pulled out a handkerchief and dabbed at his eyes.

"The Moon wants the peoples of the world to be happy and enjoy the moonlight without war that kills and maims the innocent," he concluded. As his voice trembled, he begged, "With your help, we can save the planet." Again, he looked into the eyes of the Moon Goddess.

The Sun Rays clapped but not with the vigor of the college peace crowds. Star passed around a basket and to Monica it appeared people were tossing in fives and a few tens. Star handed the basket to John who thanked one and all.

When John sat down, the Moon Goddess said to him. "That was wonderful! I know the Moon is pleased."

"Perhaps we could talk some more privately. I would love to see the Moon Room," purred John. He handed the basket to Jessica to hold.

"You are such a nice young man. Of course, let's just go over there right now. I'm sure the young ladies won't mind." John stood up, opened the door for the Moon Goddess, and left with just a brief hand wave.

Since Star was talking with the Sun Rays about transportation to the opera, and John was visiting with the Moon Goddess, the three women looked at one another and chatted about the chance for rain and other banalities.

Suddenly Jessica broke into the conversation, "Why did John talk about the sun and moon wanting harmony? They don't give a rip. They're not people."

Monica measured out her words carefully, "I think he said those things about the sun and moon because that's what these people believe."

"Who cares about their crazy ideas? We need to work for peace." Jessica was sitting straight up in her chair and bouncing her knee with nervous energy.

"Maybe he thinks he can get money out of them by pretending to believe," Monica said.

"But that's dishonest!" blurted Jessica in righteous indignation.

Sheila said dryly, "It works."

"John is not the man I thought he was," Jessica wailed. "I thought he would never stoop to get money. I know the peace movement needs money, but saying the sun and moon want peace. That's crazy!"

Monica nodded in agreement but didn't further comment because Star was walking towards them. He clasped his hands and said, "That was a beautiful speech. Everything that Mr. Spenser said fits our theme so well."

Sheila answered, "Yes, John is good at adapting to the themes of others."

"But," Star continued, "I have forgotten my manners. My deepest sympathy on the loss of Jeff Landsdon. We knew him well here at our church, and we share your grief."

"You knew him?" sputtered Sheila.

"Oh, yes, we knew him. He was our travel agent. He came to us months ago and worked on our trip to Egypt. We wanted to go there because the ancient Egyptians used to worship Ra, another name for the Sun. When we found out the name of his travel agency was Moonbeam, we knew it was fate that we should select him to plan our trip."

"Moonbeam Travel, yes, it must have been fate to find a travel agency with that name," said Sheila dryly.

"Yes, he was very accommodating. He arranged our plane tickets, hotel stays, and river cruises for 20 people. Luckily, we gave him the money last month, and so now everything is already paid in full. That sounds terrible, doesn't it. I mean it's lucky he had everything done before he died. I'm sure he wanted to finish his business before he died. Although he didn't know he was going to die, but ... " Star's tongue was getting more and more tied up while trying to say something nice about Jeff's fortuitous death after making the trip arrangements.

Sheila suddenly looked very intensely at Star. "Did you say you gave him the money to pay the airlines, hotels, etc?"

"Yes, he said it was more efficient that way," answered Star.

"I'm sure it was efficient in more ways than one," replied Sheila as she avoided his eyes and glanced out a window.

Monica looked at Sheila and wondered why she was asking these questions. She started thinking about the name Moonbeam Travel and the amount of money involved. She guessed the cost for each participant would be at least $5000 plus air fare which could be up to $4000 and times 20 would be about $180,000. Was it possible Jeff had scammed the Church of the Sun and Moon of at least $180,000?

Star Stephens added, "We got a receipt from Moonbeam Travel, but as of yet we haven't gotten our tickets. Surely in the next couple days we'll get them. We're due to leave in two weeks."

Sheila smiled and said, "Of course, you'll be getting them in a couple days." Monica. thought she saw a gleam in Sheila's eyes, sort of a now-I-know-what-he-was-up-to look.

The Moon Goddess and John reappeared. Both were smiling and John surreptitiously patted his pocket. "The Moon Room was glorious. Your church is doing a fine thing for the world. I'm glad you realize peace is so important, and you are willing to support it. I'd like to come back, if I may," purred John.

Star looked pleased as punch. He almost strutted when he said, "Of course, of course, anytime you wish."

"Star Burst, dear, this man is so wonderful. He says he's interested in our church, but he doesn't have a lot of time to spend here since his mission is so important. I agree peace is a wonderful idea," prattled the Goddess of the Moon.

John smiled broadly at the God and Goddess while he smoothed down a stray hair at the side of his face. He gave his tie a little twist, and Monica thought she could hear a little jingle from his keys as he fingered them in his pocket. Obviously John was ready to leave.

"John," Sheila said, "did you know Jeff had been in the travel business? His agency, Moonbeam Travel, prepared a trip to Egypt for Star and Mrs. Harkenstone and some of the church members. They gave him the money to make the payments for the airlines, hotels and other arrangements."

John looked startled, "Really?"

"Yes," replied Mrs. Harkenstone. "We just knew it was fate when we saw the name of his agency. And he was such a nice young man. We are so sorry about his departure from this world. Star, do you remember if he had purchased a Rapture robe? I certainly hope so. We must always be ready for you-know-what."

Star looked thoughtful, "I think he bought the #100 model in paradise green."

"Good, I'm sure the color looked good on him," said Mrs. Harkenstone. "Have you all seen our Rapture line of clothing? I'm sure you could find a style and color to fit your taste."

"Yes, I'm sure we could, but perhaps we'll wait just a few more days before we make our selections. We really have to go now," said John smoothly as he fingered his keys in his pants pocket.

Monica thought John must have taken lessons from a cat on making such agreeable, soft sounds.

As a parting gesture, Star called out, "Our Jupiter Boutique is open every day from 10 to 5 if you want to select your robes from our Rapture line. No need to call ahead."

When they were in the parking lot, John turned to Sheila. "Did you know Jeff had a Moonbeam Travel agency, and he arranged a trip for those Beams or Rays or whatevers?"

"No, that was news to me," replied Sheila.

John had a thoughtful look in his eyes, and Monica could almost hear the wheels turning in his head. She thought he was trying to connect the dots. Sheila, on the other hand, looked like she had connected the dots very quickly since her lips turned up at the edges, and her eyes sparkled.

John turned to get into his car and spoke to Monica and Sheila. "Jessica and I will meet you at the El Pinto restaurant. Randy should be meeting us there since she didn't show up at this Sun Palace or whatever it is. And, Sheila, are you sure you didn't know about this travel agency business?"

"John, would I lie to you? I didn't know a thing about it," swore Sheila.

Once Monica and Sheila were driving towards the restaurant, Sheila muttered, " I knew Jeff was up to something. Now where did he put the money?"

Monica decided to act innocent, "What do you mean, Sheila?

"It was a scam. Jeff robbed those people of at least $180,000. I was married to him. I know he could look sincere and boyish while lying. He fooled me for awhile."

"To make a successful scam, he would need letterhead stationary, brochures, and probably a fake office. How would he get the money to do all that? And where would all that stuff be?"

"I don't know, but it's got to be here in Albuquerque, and I'm going to find it before John does. I could tell his nose was twitching after he found out about Jeff's little side game."

"But the money belongs to the Church of the Sun and Moon. And it won't be long before the God and Goddess will find out they've been screwed. When the police get involved, they'll find the money and return it to them which is the right thing to do," said Monica feeling she had to express the ethical, responsible position to the morally challenged Sheila.

"Don't worry about it, honey. It doesn't concern you," said Sheila.

Monica nodded. "You're right. After dinner tonight, I'm going to head home, grade my papers, and do my lesson plans. I have enough on my plate, and all of this is none of my business."

But could she keep out of it?

II

Back at work the next day, Monica told everything that had happened the previous day to Leslie as they stood out in the hall during passing time at their high school. "Randy never showed up at the church or the restaurant afterwards. John certainly didn't seem to care, and, of course, Jessica probably was glad she wasn't there. Jessica kept saying to John the moon and sun aren't people and they don't care about peace. John changed the subject by complimenting her hair or her eyes."

"It sounds like the dinner was sort of boring. But I want to visit the Church of the Sun and Moon. This Star Burst character and the Moon Goddess seem almost unbelievable," commented Leslie.

"They're nice, crazy people. I'm almost sure they were scammed out of a lot of money, but I can't go to the police, or even Rick, until they don't get their tickets. On the other hand, it's possible Sheila just thinks Jeff took their money, and I went along with her ideas. We don't even know if the travel agency exists."

"Have you looked in the most obvious place for the Moonbeam Travel Agency?"

"You mean in the telephone book? That's an excellent idea."

The two women were interrupted by students who wanted to know if there was an assembly today. So their chat ended, and both went back to the heavy task of teaching English 12.

After the school day ended, Monica took out her telephone directory and looked under travel agencies in the yellow pages. There she found the Moonbeam Travel Agency. The address was fairly close to the school and in a strip mall. Monica went next door to tell Leslie the news. "Let's check it out. I'm really curious about all of this."

Leslie tucked her papers into her tote in preparation for her evening work. She hesitated before answering, "I've really got a stack of papers to grade, but, sure, I'll go with you."

The two of them climbed into Monica's car and drove to the strip mall which had just three small businesses: an insurance company, a wholesale paper company, and the Moonbeam Travel Agency. In the window of the travel agency, a huge paper moon shone over a beach scene with a beautiful couple embracing on a perfect, sandy beach. On the door a sign said, "I'll be back in 15 minutes."

Both of the women peered into the window, but they could see very little. They checked their watches and mentally calculated when the person would return. While they were standing there, an employee of the insurance company came over to them. "It's going to be a long wait. That sign has been there for weeks and that fellow hasn't come back."

"Do you know the owner? Do you think he's sold the business or what do you think is going on?" Monica had a dozen questions in mind.

"It wasn't much of a business. I didn't see anyone go in there. In fact most of the time the business appeared to be closed, or sometimes he put that little 15 minute sign on the door. This isn't a good location if you want any foot traffic so I don't know why he rented here in the first place."

"We heard this agency was owned by Jeff Landsdon. Have you heard that name in connection with the business?" asked Monica.

"Yes, he introduced himself one time when we were both opening our doors. I spoke to him and his secretary, Maria Garcia, a couple times later."

"He's dead so either the business has been sold or has just been abandoned," said Monica.

"Dead? He always looked fit," said the man. "Was it a heart attack? He looked like the type who might burn the candle at both ends." He shook his head in disbelief.

Monica just nodded since she didn't want to go over all the details of the murder. "What about his secretary? There are so many Garcias in Albuquerque, I'd never be able to find her in the telephone book. Do you know where she lives?

The man shook his head. "I haven't a clue."

As the two women walked back to the car, a Prius parked next to them, and John jumped out. "Hi there, is anyone in the office?"

"No one's here. The door is locked. The man next door says the office is hardly ever open," answered Monica.

"I got curious about this travel agency thing. Jeff never mentioned it to me. When Sheila picked up the dogs this morning, she said she didn't know about it either. I just decided I had to take a look so I found the address in the phone book. And by the way, a strange thing happened last night. Jeff's computer, or rather the Peace Movement's computer which he used, has been stolen from my room. Something is going on." John shook the door knob as he talked.

"A computer was stolen?"

"Yes, last night before I got back to my room. I have my own personal computer and another one for the Peace Movement which Jeff used for making arrangements for hotels, air lines, letters, etc. The police had it for awhile, and yesterday they released it. Both computers were in my suite before I left to go to that Sun and Moon church, and when I returned after taking Jessica home, one was gone. I asked the man who has his room next to mine if he heard the dogs bark. He said he was a light sleeper, but he didn't hear any barking all night."

John rattled the door knob two or three more times but finally gave up.

"Those yappy little dogs of Sheila's didn't bark?" questioned Monica.

"That's what he said."

"The dogs that didn't bark," mused Monica as she thought about an old Sherlock Holmes story.

John continued, "I wonder if Jeff was an employee or actually owned the agency. Where did he get the money if he owned it? There's a lot of mystery here."

Monica blurted out what she had been thinking, "Do you think he was a fraud? Did he scam Mrs. Harkenstone out of all that trip money?"

"No, I'm sure Jeff wouldn't do such a thing. However, he shouldn't have been working another job while he was on my payroll. The Peace Movement should have taken up all his time," John complained.

"I don't know how or when he did it, but it was a rotten thing to swindle those people," insisted Monica as she peered into the big front window. All she could see was a big brown desk, a brown and green stripped sofa and a brass coffee table with travel brochures on it.

"I wonder where the key is?" John asked as he jiggled the handle once again.

Monica offered a possible solution, "The police might still have all his keys. They probably didn't know about his agency business. We all found out just by co-incidence when we were talking to Star at the church."

"I'll speak to that Detective Rick Miller fellow. Now I have to run by the church and meet with Mrs. Harkenstone. She's such a lovely lady, and I believe she has become very interested in our peace work." John stroked his chin and smoothed his hair as he walked towards his Prius.

"Monica, I'm dying to visit this church. Do you think we could go over there now? We wouldn't have to stay long. We could visit those little shops you were telling me about," urged Leslie.

"Why not? It's not far from here. I don't know when they have services, but those little shops are open all day. If we meet up with Star, he might even show us the rest of the place. I would like to see the Moon Room where Mrs. Harkenstone reigns as the Goddess of the Moon."

Both cars left the strip mall and headed for the Church of the Sun and Moon. Leslie and Monica chatted about the travel agency. Monica commented, "It appears to me Jeff has taken the Egyptian trip money and stashed the loot some place." Leslie agreed.

By the time they arrived at the Church of the Sun and Moon, John had already gone inside. Outside in the parking lot, Leroy, the war advocate, was dragging his sign in the gravel and kicking a few loose stones with his right foot. When he saw the two women, he looked up with his puppy dog eyes and asked, "Is she here?"

"Who?" asked Monica.

"Jessica. I haven't seen her for the last few days. She's always with *him*. I know they came here yesterday. I followed her. I've really been tense, but I've been reading Hemingway for my American Lit class, and I think I'm showing 'grace under pressure.'"

"Yes, you are," affirmed Monica who felt she should always encourage students. She tried to think of another way of helping the dejected Leroy. "Would you like to go in the church and look it over? This is one church unlike all others."

"I might as well. I just finished work, and I don't have to be any place. I'd like to be with my own girl, but ... " His voice trailed off, and he kicked a couple more rocks.

"Leave your sign outside, Leroy. You can pick it up later," advised Monica.

Leroy stowed his "Kill the Evil Doers" placard behind a bush and stumbled toward the entrance with Monica and Leslie. His head, covered with a baseball cap on backwards, drooped until his chin almost touched his white tee shirt which had the words "Make War and Love."

"Maybe Star will cheer him up," whispered Monica to Leslie. Star appeared at the doorway with his cherubic smile welcoming them. He wore a different robe, a sky blue silk with a huge sun on the back in gold with sequins outlining the edges and radiating out in all directions like sun rays.

"Welcome to the Church of the Sun and Moon. May the sun warm your spirit, and may the moon comfort your dreams," said Star as he held out his hand.

"I brought some guests with me, Star. I'd like you to meet Leslie Davis who teaches with me and a University student, Leroy Marx," said Monica.

Leslie gushed, "I've heard sooo much about your beautiful church. I would love to see it all." She smiled and gave her hand to Star.

Still scowling, Leroy held out his hand, "Nice to meet you."

Star bubbled over with excitement, " Gosh, this is great. We haven't had so many visitors in ages. Yesterday we had four, and today we have two come-backs and two new ones. This church is going to grow. I told the Moon Goddess that just this morning."

"We're not ready to join yet, Star, but Leslie and Leroy would like to see the wonderful way you've decorated the building."

Bouncing along, Star led the way along the path with the large cottonwood trees and the two featured pieces of art. Leslie looked at the big moon and sun globes with the little ray things sticking out in all directions. She whispered to Monica, "I wonder who made these?"

"Probably some art major from the University who needed some extra money," Monica whispered back. Leroy's chin no longer drooped as he also stared in awe at the two large globes.

Once they were inside the building, Star pointed at the different shops. Leroy perked up when he smelled pizza . "I'm getting a little hungry. If it's alright with you, I'd like to stop in and have a slice of pepperoni," said Leroy. Monica looked at his gaunt eyes and sagging shoulders and thought perhaps he hadn't eaten for awhile.

"Maybe we all could stop for a bite," added Monica.

The group didn't hesitate at all and quickly turned into Pallas's Pizza Parlor. Star played the host and ordered a slice for all four of them. "I could use a little pick-me-up myself," said Star. "In fact, let's have a beer to go with it."

"Beer in the church building?" questioned Monica with her mouth slightly agape.

"Yes, isn't it great. I always like to have a beer when I eat pizza," said Star.

Leroy was now looking incredulously at Star in his blue silk robe talking about beer and pizza in the Church of the Sun and Moon. Leslie, too, gave Monica a what-kind-of-church-is-this look.

Star didn't seem to notice their astonishment, but busily handed out a mug of beer to everyone in the party. "To the Sun!" he said and raised his glass in the gesture of the toast.

All lifted their glasses and said in unison, "To the Sun!" Everyone took a long pull and set their glasses down.

"This is a very interesting introduction to your church," said Leslie. "Do you get many University students as members of the congregation?"

"We haven't done much recruiting or I mean, evangelizing," explained Star. "But maybe we should. I'll talk to the Moon Goddess about that idea."

John Spenser entered the Pallas. Monica thought he must have a nose for the smell of booze. He looked around and said, "I'm looking for the Moon Goddess, but she doesn't seem to be here."

"Usually she comes in the late afternoon. She should be here soon but come over and have a beer while you're waiting," invited Star while he wiped his chin with his hand.

John sat down at the table and accepted a beer from Star. "How are things going?" asked Leslie.

John leaned back and took a swallow of beer. " I don't know how to answer that question. Things are going great with my peace movement. I have a number of speaking engagements coming up, and here in Albuquerque, I've had a huge response. But I've had this terrible threat on my life, and until the criminal is caught, my life is always in danger."

Monica said, "It was the best of times, it was the worst of times."

"That's a very good comment," said John as he looked at her.

"It's not mine. Charles Dickens said it," replied Monica.

"Does he write for the Times?"

"No, he's been dead for awhile. He wrote a lot of good stuff. That line was from *A Tale of Two Cities*," explained Monica dryly.

"Ah, the Twin Cities, Minneapolis and St. Paul. Two lovely cities together in Minnesota. I"ve been there several times."

"Actually, Charles Dickens wrote about London and Paris," said Monica while trying not to sound too pompous.

"All great cities. And, of course, Albuquerque also is a great city," added John.

Star burped and piped up, "I think the Sun especially loves Albuquerque because we have sunshine every single day. Let's drink to the Sun!" Everyone lifted their glasses again and took another swig.

At this point the waiter brought out the hot pizza and a pitcher of beer. Star filled his empty glass and passed the pitcher along. Everyone munched pizza and slurped more beer.

When John saw the Moon Goddess enter, he got up from his chair, walked over to her, and said, "How lovely you look tonight!"

"Thank you, dear boy. I'm wearing my new gown. I have one for every phase of the moon in seed pearls, and Melody designed another with black silk and sequins. I like the silver sequins myself."

"I'd like to talk to you some more about my peace movement. Would you like to take a seat over at this table? I'm sure the group would allow us a little privacy for our talk." He pulled out a chair for her at an empty table.

The Moon Goddess waved at the pizza eaters, swished across the room, and sat down at the offered chair. After she was properly seated, John asked, "Would you like coffee, a soft drink, a beer?"

"Beer, thank you, dear boy." The waiter was on his way before she even got the word out of her mouth. Evidently he knew the Moon Goddess liked to toss back a few.

John leaned towards Mrs. Harkenstone and murmured, "The sequins in your gown bring out the beauty of your eyes." She smiled and gave her hair a little fluff. "Your skin is radiant. It truly makes you the essence of a Moon Goddess."

The small room allowed the four pizza eaters to be in earshot of John's supposedly private conversation. When Leslie and Monica heard these outrageous words of flattery, they both gave a simultaneous eye roll. Leroy stopped chewing, and even Star turned his head toward the other table. No one spoke or chewed.

John continued with his sweet talk, "Moon Goddess, the night becomes you; it brings out your incandescence. You light up the sky."

Monica wondered if he had prepared his little speech since he used a word like "incandescence."

While Mrs. Harkenstone basked in the sound of his words, she softly giggled and cooed, "Oh, John, you dear boy, you mustn't talk like that."

Monica translated her words to mean, "Keep going."

And he did keep going. "Your beauty hangs upon the cheek of night/ Like a rich jewel in an Ethiop's ear."

"My god!" thought Monica, "Now he's using a line from Shakespeare's *Romeo and Juliet*. He must have spent quite a bit of time in preparation. Using this quote is really too much."

The Moon Goddess appeared to be eating it up while he dished it out. She gave a sigh of contentment and oozed warmth and affection towards John who kept looking into her eyes while maintaining an expression of sincerity. "The moon, I believe, is more important than the sun. It controls so many things. For instance more babies are born during a full moon."

When the Sun God overheard that last remark, he cleared his throat and announced loud enough so the other table would be sure to hear him, "The sun makes all things grow. Without the sun, the earth would be barren."

Both John and Mrs. Harkenstone lifted their heads and looked up at Star. John spoke magnanimously, "Both the sun and the moon are necessary for our wonderful life here on earth."

Leroy said, "We get 'lunatic' from the Latin word for moon. I guess the moon brings out insanity."

Mrs. Harkenstone's eyes turned cold as she glared at Leroy. Her voice sharpened as she reprimanded Leroy, "Young man, we don't use words like that here!" The terrible word "lunatic" broke John's spell. The Moon Goddess reached out for her beer and had another swallow. Everyone followed her example.

John coughed and said, "A few cranks just made up that connection. It really doesn't apply to the moon." Mrs. Harkenstone didn't appear to be mollified because she still was sucking up her beer while darting her eyes over at Leroy. Monica thought Leroy certainly seemed to enjoy being controversial.

"I'll be back in a moment," said the Moon Goddess who picked up a corner of her black silk skirt and left. While the pizza eaters finished off their food, Monica noticed John was fumbling in his pocket. He brought out a small mirror, took a quick look, adjusted a stray hair, and slid it back in his pocket.

When the Moon Goddess returned, she announced, "Let's all go up to the Moon Room." Everyone wiped crumbs off their laps, pushed their chairs back, and tossed paper napkins and empty plates in the trash.

Monica opened her purse and glanced around for a bill. Star said, "The treat's on us." Everyone murmured their thanks and followed the Moon Goddess as she climbed the stairs.

Monica had anticipated the Moon Room would be as fanciful and as grand as the Sun Room. It was. The black painted chairs faced a huge white circle on the wall illuminated by hundreds of tiny lights sprinkled over the surface. Monica blinked at the brilliance On a dias, three steps above the floor, a huge throne style chair covered in a silver embroidered tapestry dominated the room. The Goddess's special seat rose higher than the Sun God's. This beautiful throne would fit in King Louis XVI's palace.

Wearing a dreamy expression on her face, the Moon Goddess sat in her chair and indicated with a gracious gesture others should sit, too. Each black painted wooden chair had a soft, comfortable dark pad. The Moon Goddess punched a button on her arm rest, and the lights on the wall formed a crescent. Another button push and the lights shone a different phase of the moon.

"Quite a light show," said Monica.

"Yes, I enjoy it. Sometimes I go through all the phases several times. I find it very relaxing."

The Moon Goddess pressed another button and small lights attached to the molding at the bottom of the walls came on. "I installed those so people wouldn't stumble."

The spectators waited for the Goddess to speak. After she wiggled a bit to get comfy, she began. "I want to tell you a little bit about our church, and if you have questions, I will be happy to answer them. We worship the sun and the moon. We take turns and have alternate services since the day is divided into day and night. Both are necessary for our world. Wouldn't you agree, Sun God?"

The Sun God nodded in affirmation and added, "Sometimes we have a sunset service and worship both on the same day. Those are our special feast days, and afterwards we have a big dinner and drink champagne. On our last feast day, we had cup cakes decorated to fit each part of the day: half with chocolate and the other half with yellow frosting."

"Any questions?"asked the Moon Goddess after this intellectual explication of the theology of her church. While Leslie shook her head back and forth, Monica shot a brief look at Leroy. She hoped he wouldn't ask any questions that dealt with the "lunatic" word.

Monica decided to ask about the trip since she was curious about the amount of money Jeff might have stolen from Mrs. Harkenstone. "How many people are going to Egypt to hear about Ra?"

"We will be a party of 20. All our congregation members wanted to go, and so, of course, I want to pay their way. It will be a wonderful trip. Mr. Landsdon arranged the airline, the hotels, the trip down the Nile, and all the lectures on Ra." The Moon Goddess added, "I'm so sorry about his passing on. He was a great help to us."

Monica liked this generous and goofy lady. She thought that this trip to Egypt must cost her over $180,000, and now it appeared John was buttering up the old woman to make a few fast bucks, too. As far as she knew, John hadn't taken any money, but she felt he was about to pounce otherwise he wouldn't make these outrageous compliments. Star Burst seemed to be gullible, likeable, and goofy, too. What a pair. As she sat there, she decided she would tell Rick all about it. He knew about bunko, or whatever you call deception to make money.

John spoke to the Moon Goddess. "The moon gives us peaceful slumber. Let's make sure everyone in the world can enjoy that peace. Perhaps we could have a group here at the church who could work for peace. They could be called Moon Beams for Peace."

"I like that. Moon Beams for Peace is a wonderful name. Yes, I think we should do that, don't you Sun God?"

The Sun God nodded affirmatively. Monica wondered if the Sun God ever went against the moneyed Goddess. Probably not. It was in his best interest to keep her happy, and although he seemed to be a simple fellow, he must have good instincts for keeping the status quo.

John pressed on, "Perhaps a small donation could start the group. What do you think about tee shirts with Moon Beams for Peace in white on a black background?"

The Moon Goddess wrinkled her forehead in thought. "Maybe a crescent moon in the center with the words underneath. Yes, a black tee shirt would be best. Would you be willing to take care of all the details? I could give you $1000 to order the tee shirts and to cover any other expenses."

"I would be most happy to take care of the details for you. I want to get the best quality of tee shirt. Could you make out the check for a little more, $1500 or $2000? The money is for a good cause."

"Yes, of course, dear boy. I don't want to be stingy. The moon wants everyone in the world to sleep in peace, just as you mentioned earlier. I like that. Let's put it on a tee shirt, too." The Moon Goddess's eyes sparkled as she considered the words and colors for the new tee shirts.

"Excellent, Goddess, you are very creative. I'll have an artist design both ideas you suggested. I'll check with you, of course, before they're printed."

"Yes, yes," sighed Mrs. Harkenstone while she wrote a $3000 check to John.

John pocketed the check, smiled at her, and said, "You are helping many people sleep in peace, dear goddess."

Leroy chimed in, "The best way to let the world sleep in peace is to kill the evil doers." Monica thought Leroy just didn't know when to keep his mouth shut.

The Moon Goddess, however, wasn't offended since she didn't reprimand the young whippersnapper but merely shrugged her shoulders. He did get a sharp glance from John, but no words. Monica decided that although Leroy could be annoying, he was so ineffectual no one made any big effort to squelch him. However, she felt If he said the "lunatic" word again Mrs. Harkenstone would give him a good tongue lashing.

Star invited the group to see the Sun Room and the little shops on the first floor. Everyone stood up except John and Mrs. Harkenstone. "I'd like to talk some more to the Moon Goddess about our peace movement," said John. As the group walked out, Monica noticed John had inched his chair closer to the throne so he could speak in a more intimate way to his benefactress.

Leslie enjoyed the tour and praised Star for the beautiful decorations. They stopped at Jupiter's Boutique to see the Rapture line of clothing.

When Melody saw Star, she ran over to him and said, "I'm so excited! I just heard Rev. Plankton has predicted the world is ending Nov. 3. Isn't that good news? That's just about a month away. When I called him up, I said I would be happy to bring my collection of Rapture clothes to his church for a private showing. He agreed if we give him 20% of the sale, so tomorrow I'm going over there, and I bet we'll sell quite a few. Isn't that fabulous? Star, you should tell your members so they can get their robes now while we still have a good selection."

Monica and Leslie didn't want to hurt Melody's feelings so they looked at the robes and made complimentary comments about their beauty. "I'm not ready to buy one now," murmured Monica.

"Don't wait too long. We now have a definite date. I think I'll have to fatten my inventory since there'll probably be a run on the heavenly-white-with-pearls number," added Melody who was counting her inventory as she spoke.

"What if Rev. Plankton is wrong?" piped up Leroy.

Melody got a thoughtful expression on her face as if she hadn't considered that possibility before. "I guess we just keep on going. But let's look on the bright side."

The three visitors thanked Star for his tour and left him to discuss with Melody the number of the celestial blues and the paradise purples that will be needed. Monica almost felt naughty enough to ask if they had given the fiery reds a good think.

Once in the parking lot, Leroy picked up his placard and got into his own car. Leslie waited until she and Monica returned to the Prius, before she spoke, "What a crazy place! I've never seen anything like it. And I've never met any people like them before."

"They're all rather sweet," said Monica. "I really don't think Melody paid off Rev. Plankton. She seemed to be sincerely surprised with his announcement; however, not many people would be as happy as she with an end of the world date."

Leslie giggled, "Great news! The end of the world is coming November 3."

They both cracked up at this incongruity. Monica howled so much a few tears came to her eyes. After they both stopped laughing, Monica started the car, and they left the Church of the Sun and the Moon. Monica wondered if Jeff had taken advantage of the naivete of the chubby royalty of the universe. Tomorrow she would do more investigating.

12

Later that evening, Monica and Rick sipped coffee and ate hot apple pie with vanilla ice cream at the Flying Star restaurant. Since the weather was beautiful, they had chosen to sit outside in the little patio. Rick looked at her and said, "I'm so glad you called me tonight."

"I had all this information about Jeff Landsdon I felt you should know. It might have nothing to do with his murder, but I wanted to tell you anyway."

"Information of any kind is good in a murder case. I have a few ideas about it, but nothing definite. I don't necessarily think John Spenser was the intended victim."

Monica used her spoon to scrape the melted ice cream off her plate before she answered, "I had that idea myself. When I heard Jeff had arranged this trip to Egypt through a travel agency called Moonbeam, and Mrs. Harkenstone said she knew it was fate for her to choose his agency because of the name, I got suspicious. When Leslie and I went there and found out it was closed most of the time, I thought it was a scam. Do you remember meeting Sheila, his wife? She immediately came to that conclusion. But so far the Sun group believes everything has been paid, and they're all set. Can you find out what is going on?" After blurting out all her thoughts, Monica took another sip of coffee.

"I'll try," said Rick. "I hope Mrs. Harkenstone's group hasn't been swindled, but I agree with you there are suspicious circumstances." He stirred his coffee and with a small chuckle asked, " Do you read many detective novels?"

"Oh, all the time. I particularly like the ones that have a woman who likes to investigate crime. Usually when she talks to the police detective about her ideas on the case, he tries to get rid of her for being nosy and annoying."

"You definitely are not annoying. I like hearing what you have to say." He kept smiling and looked at her with soft eyes. A lock of Rick's hair fell over his forehead which Monica thought was very attractive.

"Sheila keeps looking for Jeff's big stash of money which she says belongs to her, but if he stole the money, then it isn't hers. And, of course, there might not be any money. Larry keeps hanging around and keeps asking John for his money. Money seems to be a big concern for some of these people," said Monica as she started to philosophize.

"It's one of the main motives for murder," added Rick.

"Money buys power and status," mused Monica, "but often results in loss of integrity and happiness. Literature is full of that theme: man gains wealth and loses his soul."

"That theme is in *Macbeth,* one of my favorite plays," said Rick. "After Macbeth murders Duncan so he can become king, he has no joy in life. 'O, full of scorpions is my mind.' is a line which describes to me exactly what a tortured soul would suffer."

" I love that play; it's part of the curriculum in English 12 so I teach it every year. I'm so glad you like Shakespeare."

"Maybe as a policeman, I like to think no one really profits from crime. And that play has great scenes which point out how guilt can drive a person insane. Remember the one in which he sees the dead Banquo, the friend that he had killed, at his state dinner. Guilt can cause all sorts of reactions, and that scene has a lot of power."

"I just love that scene, too, and the one when guilt finally takes away Lady Macbeth's sanity. At first she urges her husband to kill the king, but later she keeps seeing blood on her hands. Everyone remembers when she tries to wash off the imaginary blood from her hands and says, 'Out, damned spot!' Later she believes the smell of blood will always be with her when she says, 'All the perfumes of Arabia will not sweeten this little hand.'"

Rick said, "Yes, those were great lines. I liked the scenes with the witches. Do you remember that line when Macbeth is approaching, and one of the witches says, 'By the pricking of my thumbs/ Something wicked this way comes'"

"And, of course, everyone likes the time when the three witches gather around the fire and put snakes, newts, eyes, and other gross stuff in the big pot as they prepare the charm," said Monica as she leaned forward in her chair.

Immediately both of them said in unison, "'Double, double, toil and trouble/ Fire burn and caldron bubble.'" Then they laughed delightedly together. The evening continued until the restaurant closed.

The next day Monica told Leslie about the evening she spent with Rick. "We talked about the case, and he isn't that convinced John Spenser was the intended victim. I had that same thought. He's going to find out about the financing for the Egyptian trip because he, too, thinks fraud could be involved. Then we talked about ethics. Can you believe a police detective likes Shakespeare. He even quoted lines. You know he really is a very nice person."

Leslie cocked her head a little. "Ah ha, I think it's not just the Landsdon case that interests you. Perhaps, a certain detective?"

Monica blushed and grinned. Their conversation ended when the bell rang for class and both the women turned to go into their classrooms.

At the end of the school day when the kids had emptied the room, Monica went next door to see Leslie. "I think we should talk to Sheila again. She's chatty, and we could find out some more about Jeff."

" I have tons of work to do, and I can't take the time to run off and talk to people about Jeff. Take a break from it."

"Perhaps I am getting a little overly involved, but it interests me. Maybe I'll just give Sheila a ring, and if she wants to go have a beer or a cup of coffee,

I could spend just a little time with her. She doesn't know many people here, and she may want to talk with someone."

Monica pulled out her cell phone and poked in her number. After a few minutes of talking, she hung up and called out to Leslie, "See you tomorrow. I'm off to have coffee with Sheila at the hotel."

Sheila and her dogs were sitting at an outdoor umbrella table in the patio when Monica arrived at the hotel. Each dog sat in a chair and lapped water out of her own plastic bowl. Both dogs made yappy noises in a staccato rhythm when they saw Monica. Sheila stifled a yawn and mumbled in a monotone, "Stop it, you two." They didn't stop yipping until she petted each shiny little head. "I took them for a walk, and now they're a little tired and cranky," explained Sheila.

Monica didn't notice any different behavior than usual. They always barked and jumped around, but at the same time, they were always cute. She sat down and poured a cup of hot coffee from a carafe on the table and asked, "How are things going?"

"Not much has happened. I called a number of the storage companies and asked if Jeff Landsdon had rented a unit from them. Most said they couldn't reveal that information. The others just said he hadn't. I think he used another name."

"Perhaps, he didn't rent any storage unit. Perhaps there isn't any money. Perhaps he was an honest business man trying to make a few extra bucks while being on John's payroll," suggested Monica. while she sipped her coffee.

Sheila stretched out her legs, shook her head, and answered, "I know him. I lived with the jerk." Their private conversation was interrupted by the sudden arrival of John who looked very informal in jean shorts and a golf polo shirt.

"Hello, you two," shouted John as he breezed over to their table. "And how are the little furry friends today?" he added while they barked and spilled their water from all their energetic frenzy.

"Stop it," crooned Sheila to the dogs in her usual perfunctory way. She turned to John, "Sit down, John. How are you?"

"I'm great. I'm going to check on the designs for the tee shirts Mrs. Harkenstone wants for her congregation. I called a company, and they have prepared several examples so I can show them to her when I see her tonight. I'm going to the opera with her group." John leaned back in the chair and smiled expansively.

"You're going to the opera!" squeaked Sheila and then dissolved into a fit of laughter. Monica discreetly looked down and started mopping up the spilled water with paper napkins. At seeing their mother snorting and squealing, the dogs jumped on the table and danced in circles while emitting little yelps. Monica quickly reached for her coffee before they could knock it over.

While all this hilarity was going on, John inhaled and spit out in a cold voice, "It isn't that funny, Sheila. I've been to the opera before. It may not be my favorite form of entertainment, but I plan on enjoying myself tonight."

Sheila recovered enough to get the dogs off the table and to settle each one down on a chair. "Sorry, I just couldn't see you voluntarily going to an opera."

John sniffed and said, "It's *The Magic Flute* and should be very good."

Monica chimed in, "Mrs. Harkenstone mentioned that the Queen of the Night sings one of her favorite arias. But I'm sure she's told you about it. I like that opera too. I saw it a couple years ago in Chicago."

Sheila recovered from her fit of merriment and got down to business. "John, what was Jeff up to?"

"I don't think he was up to anything. Jeff was a good guy although he shouldn't have been working another job while he was on my payroll."

"Time will tell since the Egyptian trip is coming up in a couple weeks. By the way, what are you going to do with the rest of the $3000 after you pay for the tee shirts?"

"The money, of course, will be used for bringing peace to the world. You are so suspicious of everyone. And I, of course, should be suspicious because my life is in danger. Any day I could be murdered by this insane person. I hope the police will find him or her soon. This pressure is affecting my complexion. Notice how pale and wan I look." John whipped out his pocket mirror and studied his face.

Sheila wickedly said, "You're right, John, you aren't looking good at all."

John immediately squinted into the mirror and intensely checked out his forehead, cheeks, and chin.

"Do you see any worry lines, fatigue discolorations, or God forbid, pimples?" he asked.

Monica shifted from watching John's close inspection of his face to seeing a gleeful look in Sheila's eyes.

"You're looking a little sallow. I'm worried about how this whole thing is affecting you," continued Sheila.

"You're right, I do look a bit peaked," he mumbled. He pulled down the skin from under one eye and scrutinized the area. "Do you see any redness at the corner of the eye ball?"

Monica decided to join in the fun. "Just a little pink, and I agree with Sheila. Your skin coloring is a little off. Maybe you need more sleep."

John tried different lighting by slanting the mirror in various positions. "I see a little yellowish greenish spot on my left temple. Maybe I should be in the sun more," muttered John as he kept on turning the mirror and scrunching his muscles this way and that way. "Perhaps I'll play a little tennis tomorrow."

"With all that you're going through, I don't think anything will help," responded Sheila while shaking her head back and forth in a manner suggesting there was no hope.

Evidently John no longer wanted to study his waning looks, because he pocketed his mirror and stood up. He didn't say a word but just waved a good-bye. His bouncy walk was gone; he drooped a bit as he made his way to his car.

As soon as he was out of earshot, Sheila started to chuckle. "Sometimes I just can't resist giving him a couple barbs. He's so conceited. I enjoy knocking him down a peg or two."

Monica nodded in agreement. "I had fun too." Both of them giggled in their conspiracy. The dogs jumped on the table again, wagged their tails, and joined in the merriment. "What I can't understand is why women go for him. Jessica, Randy, and now old Mrs. Harkenstone."

"It's somewhat of a mystery. Randy has stuck with him for years. After every indiscretion, she takes him back. But this time, I think she's sick and tired of his infidelities. I talked with her this morning, and she seemed really pissed."

"How long has Randy been his girlfriend?" asked Monica.

"For years. She was with him before he started the peace movement. She helped him with all of his businesses and took care of him, almost mothered him. And the big jerk ran over her again and again. But, I sense something has changed. This Jessica thing might be the straw that breaks the camel's back."

"What a shame she's given him so much of her time and love," commiserated Monica.

"Yes," muttered Sheila, "I know exactly how dumb we women can be. But now, I'm free. I just have to think the way he used to think so I can find his money and get back what's due me."

"Were there any good times?" asked Monica who wanted to find out all she could about Jeff since a person's character could give a hint about later criminal activities.

"At first, he used to send me flowers and ice cream cakes. I loved the mocha with chocolate fudge icing the best. He called me cute names, like Boobs and Whistles because he said my figure would draw whistles from any red blooded male." After Sheila said that, she suddenly got a thoughtful expression on her face. "Boobsandwhistles, could that be it?"

Monica stared at Sheila who appeared to be lost in some memory. While Sheila wrinkled her forehead in thought, Rhonda and Stephanie jumped down from their chairs and chased each other around the table. Sheila didn't even attempt to say anything to them. Her words never had any effect, but she usually said something so the people around her would think she was a good dog mother.   .

While Sheila spaced out, Monica glanced up and saw Leroy trudging towards them dragging one of his placards. He waved his free hand, and Monica beckoned him to come over. "Do you ever go any place without your signs?" she asked.

Leroy grinned sheepishly. "I want people to know where I stand, but maybe I overdo it a bit. Jessica tells me I'm a war monger. Is she here? I've been looking for her all day."

"I haven't seen her today, Leroy. But maybe she doesn't like it you're always stalking her," advised Monica.

"You're right. I tend to overdo everything," sighed Leroy, who leaned his placard on the table. The little dogs started sniffing it, and Stephanie peed directly on the pole. When Leroy saw what was happening, he sighed again. "That's how my life is going. It represents how the world treats me."

Sheila came to life and scolded little Stephanie in her usual way. She turned to Leroy. "Let me buy you a beer. That's the least I could do after Stephanie's misbehavior. Usually she's such a good dog." Sheila picked her up and stroked her soft fur while the little nose sniffed the air.

"Sure, I could use a beer. The waiter will probably spill it in my lap. Life sucks," whined Leroy.

Sheila offered a beer to Monica, too. She offered a little hope for Leroy, "John is going to the opera tonight with Mrs. Harkenstone, and he isn't taking Jessica. Does that make you feel better?"

Leroy perked up a bit. "Huh? Are you sure?"

"Yes, I'm sure." Sheila tossed her blond hair back but didn't make any explanation to Leroy about how she had that knowledge. Changing the conversation, Sheila said, "Some of the Oz folks are still here. I talked to a couple witches last night who said they were going to stay for another week because they were having so much fun. Most of the Dorothys are gone, but I did see one this morning at breakfast and, of course, my dogs spotted her Toto. The Wizard said perhaps next year they'd make the convention last two weeks."

"Maybe I could get some of them interested in my war movement," said Leroy. "I hate being the only one at these peace movements who wants to kill the evil doers."

"Who knows? Maybe you could get some of them to help you protest," mused Sheila as she stifled a yawn. "Some of those guys will do anything."

The waiter set down the glasses of foamy beer. Sheila took hers and poured a little beer into each dog bowl. "Let's drink to Jeff," she suggested in a clear voice while under her breath she added, "and to the money I'm going to get from him."

All three lifted their mugs and said, "To Jeff." All drank including the two dogs that were lapping their beer with gusto.

"By the way, Leroy, how old are you? No one has carded you, and I've seen you drink before. I even gave you a glass of wine at my house." Monica suddenly wrinkled her forehead as she thought about underage drinking and her irresponsibility.

"I have a card that says I'm 21, but I'm really only 19 ½," confessed Leroy as he took a quaff of beer. "Everyone at the U drinks. As soon as they walk on the campus, they feel they have the right to do what college students have always done. Drink beer."

"How true," said Sheila and Monica together as they shrugged their shoulders.

Off to the left Leroy spotted a couple witches drinking beer at another table. "I'm going to ask them if they want to kill the tyrants." He took his beer and sauntered over to them. Although Monica and Sheila couldn't hear what he was saying, he must have gotten some positive reception because he sat down at the table.

Monica had barely switched her eyes from watching Leroy's progress when she saw Randy strolling towards the table. Randy looked chic in a short denim skirt and white top with turquoise necklace and earrings. She plopped down on a chair, looked at the two women, and asked, "Where's the bastard?"

Sheila started to giggle again. "He's going to the opera!"

Monica figured Sheila didn't need any clarification of the identity of the "bastard." All three women laughed, but Sheila seemed to get the biggest kick out of imagining John sitting through an opera because she was snorting and squealing again with even more enthusiasm. The dogs jumped on the table once more to join in the fun. Beer was spilled, and Monica sopped up the liquid with more paper napkins. Everyone was having a grand time.

Although Monica enjoyed talking with the two women, she didn't gain any information about the case. She was disappointed. Tomorrow was a big outside rally for peace. Maybe she'd find out something so she would have an excuse to call Rick.

13

The big peace rally was set for 4:00 at the University. A makeshift stage had been rigged at one end of the open space. Behind it rose large banners with peace signs. The students, all clad in jeans or jean shorts, were talking and glancing about as they looked for friends. In order to make a half way decent fanfare, Jessica ran up the two steps of the stage, clapped her hands, and shouted, "Let's give a big, peace cheer for John Spenser!" Everyone pounded their hands together, stamped their feet, and whistled. Monica, who was standing off to one side, was impressed.

Holding his arms up and his fingers shaped in the peace sign, John Spenser sprinted up to the stage, hugged Jessica, and exclaimed, " Let's bring peace to the world!" More applause, more foot stomping. He moved his arms back and forth, keeping the peace sign in his fingers intact. The students followed his example and swayed with him.

John shouted out, "Do we want peace?"

The students shouted, "Yes! Yes! Peace." While all this excitement was going on, Monica looked over the crowd. More students were coming as they heard all the commotion. The Moonbeams for Peace wore their new tee shirts. Although they looked a little dazed, they responded with "yeses" along with the rest.

After the cheering subsided, John began his spiel. He began by telling them about the horrors of war. At intervals, he paused so Jessica could lead them in the refrain, "We want peace now!" Jessica probably had been a cheerleader in high school because she was doing a great job of stirring them up and yet keeping them unified in the chant. She looked cute as she bounced around in jean shorts and white tee shirt.

After 10 or 15 minutes, Monica noticed another group coming up from behind. Leroy waved a huge placard with the words, "Nuke the Tyrants." Following him were five green faced people with pointy black hats and black robes. Each carried a "Witches for War" placard. The small coven walked in wavering lines.

Now and then a witch would use the pole of his placard as a broom stick and pretend to ride it. When the witches got too unruly, Leroy turned and muttered something to them. They stopped clowning for a minute or two. Then one witch went behind Leroy and mocked his drudging walk. All guffawed. Following this example, each witch mimiced his stomp- stomp plodding which led to more laughter.

Leroy turned around and pleaded, "Come on, you guys, you gotta get serious." He took off his baseball hat and wiped his brow with the back of his hand and stuck the cap back on with its brim in the back.

 The head witch took off his hat, wiped his brow, and imitated Leroy in a falsetto, "Come on, you guys, you gotta get serious." The coven convulsed in new laughter. The students looked at the witches who all took a bow which made everyone smile, except Jessica and John. They were not amused.

"Leroy, you idiot. Stop it!" shrieked Jessica with her hands on her hips. "You're ruining John's talk!"

"But war can stop evil. I'm not immoral," answered Leroy in a plaintive voice.

The head witch put his hands on his hips and said in a falsetto, "Leroy, you idiot. Stop it!" This broke up the coven again and even a few students started to laugh. The peace rally was turning into a farce.

John said to Jessica, "Pass around the donation basket." She gave a final glare at Leroy and gave a basket to each of her friends who walked through the crowd. The students were tossing in ones and fives; this was not a big money crowd. The Moonbeams walked away without throwing in a dime.

The witches picked up their signs, waved them a couple times, and used them as broomsticks to gallop in circles. The students clapped at their antics while laughing. Leroy gave up on trying to control his fellow protestors and walked over to Jessica.

Monica couldn't hear what they were saying, but very soon Leroy was dragging his sign and his feet towards her. His camouflage pants sagged, his head sagged, and even his baseball hat appeared to sag. Monica said in a soothing voice, "I think John is leaving next week. Things will be better then."

"She'll never love me again. What am I going to do?" he asked Monica.

Monica cleared her throat and advised, "Go back to the dorm and study for the rest of the week. Don't call Jessica until after John is gone. I think then she'll be ready to return to campus life, and maybe you could take her out to dinner at a nice restaurant."

Leroy dug his toe into the dirt. "I don't think I could study much now."

"Of course, you could. Just open a book and try," encouraged Monica who reverted to being a teacher. While Monica had been talking to Leroy, the witches capered on. A journalism student who worked on the college newspaper appeared with a camera. The witches posed with their signs up like flags and then as broomsticks. Most of the students were watching them and ignoring the money appeal for peace.

John made an attempt to get the audience's attention by shouting, "We want peace now!" Jessica picked up the cue and chanted with him while trying to get others to join. Into this melee two small dogs in pink sweaters raced across the grass. Their leashes trailed them as they dashed towards the green faced, black attired people.

"Stephanie, Rhonda, come back here!" shouted a tall blonde woman who was bounding after them. The dogs barked at the witches, changed course, and scampered towards John who looked at them and then at Sheila who was jogging toward her errant animals. By the time she reached the dogs and snatched their leashes, she was out of breath. "Sorry about that, John, but they just got away from me. I came down here because I heard you were going to speak again."

"I just finished. But you're not too late for the witches' show," he said dryly as he pointed at the black figures.

She turned around and glanced at the capering coven. "Why are the witches here?"

"I don't know," John huffed. He jerked his head towards Leroy. "I'm guessing he had something to do with it."

"Poor Leroy. John, you really shouldn't have interfered in that romance. But let's forget all of that. I have some news for you. The police went over to the Moonbeam Travel Agency and found it had been burglarized."

"What?" blurted out Monica who had been eavesdropping on their conversation. "Did they toss the place?" Monica hoped she used the right police lingo. She left Leroy and sidled over to John and Sheila so she could get more information.

Sheila turned her head towards Monica. "Yes, I was just there a few minutes ago at the same time the police and Detective Miller entered the building. I peeked in and saw the mess. The window by the front door had been broken, the file cabinets had been dumped out, and the stuffed chairs had been split and their stuffing spilled all over the floor. Pieces of glass were everywhere."

The man who works next door came over and told the police he had heard noises next door in the Moonbeam office when he came into work early about 6:00 a.m. He just thought the office was going to open again. When he heard a door slam, he looked out the window and saw a dark figure walk by. He couldn't identify it at all."

"What does that mean? Jeff is dead. Could there have been money someplace in the Moonbeam Travel Agency?" Monica asked Sheila.

John chimed in, "Why would anyone want to get into an abandoned office?"

"The police are investigating any business that Moonbeam Travel has done, and, of course, that would mean they're going to check up on the travel plans of Mrs. Harkenstone and her group." Sheila was brimming with news, which made Monica a little envious. She thought Rick should have called her.

"What could this burglary mean?" asked John as he scratched his head.

"Someone is very interested in what Jeff had been doing before he died," said Monica in a matter of fact voice as she nodded her head up and down in an affirming gesture.

Sheila had to keep the two leashes from twisting, but she kept on talking. "The man next door stayed in his office during lunch, and it wasn't until this afternoon when he walked out the front door that he saw the broken front window and called the police."

"Did they find any fingerprints?" asked Monica.

"The tech guy was there, but he didn't find many prints. They think the burglar used gloves. They found one piece of paper stuck to the side of a drawer. It was a sheet of stationary with Moonbeam Travel Agency printed at the top. They're going to try to trace it."

"Sheila, you really found out a lot of stuff. How did you happen to be there when the police came?" inquired Monica.

"Well," Sheila paused and took a little time to do some dog leash adjusting again as Stephanie and Rhonda were constantly moving back and forth around her legs. "I just thought I would go over there and talk to the man in the insurance company. He might know something useful."

John's eyes were now roaming around and watching the collection baskets. He cleared his throat and said, "I'm sure the police won't find any incriminating evidence. Jeff was a good man." He turned suddenly and strolled towards Jessica who was counting out bills.

"I'm going over to the office to see if the police are still there," announced Monica. She wanted to see the messed up office for herself and talk with Rick. When she glanced up, she realized Leroy had disappeared along with the witches. By now the crowd had cleared and the area looked like a typical college day with groups of twos and threes walking to class or heading to some other campus place.

Sheila walked with Monica to her car. They both chattered on about the strangeness of it all, but Monica noticed Sheila seemed perkier than she had been the day before. The dogs danced around, sniffing here and there. Occasionally Sheila had to tug on their leashes, but in general they kept close to her.

"I may be leaving in a day or two," declared Sheila, "since I've decided Jeff didn't have any money hidden. Maybe John is right, and he wasn't involved in any criminal activity."

Monica looked at her in complete surprise. "Really?" she blurted out.

"Yes, I've changed my mind," Sheila said sweetly and sauntered over to her car.

As Monica drove away, she kept thinking about Sheila's reversal. She wondered what had happened to make Sheila switch her feelings about Jeff. She had been so insistent Jeff was involved in some scheme, and today she wasn't. Very unusual. Also, she seemed happier which didn't make any sense.

The police were still combing the Moonbeam Travel Agency when Monica pulled up to the curb. As she got out of the car, Rick saw her and waved. Monica hustled over to speak to him. "Hi, Rick."

"My favorite girl detective. It's good to see you," he replied as he gave her a soft smile.

"I could say I was in the neighborhood and thought I'd just drop by, but you'd see through that. I'm just plain old nosy." As she confessed, she smiled back at him.

"It looks like someone is looking for something, but we don't know who or what or why. The burglar took whatever was in the desk." He stroked his chin and cocked his head toward her. "What do you think? Any ideas?"

Monica, thrilled he had asked her opinion, felt she had to make an intelligent guess. "Someone knows about the swindle and wants to find out where he hid the money."

"If there is a stash, it's not in his bank account. All he has is about $1500. Probably his wife will have to pay any existing bills out of it, and she'll keep the rest. Unless, of course, there is more money, and he was involved in a travel scam."

"At one time Sheila thought he stole money from Mrs. Harkenstone and might have hidden it in a storage unit, but now she told me she thinks he might have been a legitimate business man."

Rick lifted an eyebrow. "So she changed her mind. Interesting."

"It is quite strange." Monica looked into Rick's eyes as she was speaking. His eyes certainly were a warm shade of brown.

Rick added, "Another odd thing is the laptop John Spenser reported stolen was found in his closet by the hotel maid. He swore he had not misplaced it, and it really had been taken."

"So the laptop was either never stolen or someone returned it. But to change the subject, do you know anymore about the travel agency's financial transactions?" blurted out Monica who was so curious she didn't stop to think perhaps she shouldn't have asked.

"We have some information from the bank. I'll tell you all about it if you have time for a cup of coffee with me?"

"Yes, yes, I will," stuttered Monica as she felt a flush rise in her cheeks. She fingered an earring to hide her embarrassment. He took her arm and the two walked toward a little café down the street.

After the coffee and chocolate cake with fudge frosting were served, Rick filled her in on the finances of the Moonbeam Travel Agency. "Over the past six weeks there were five large checks from Mrs. Harkensone. Each check was for $45,000, but only $15,000 was put into the account. That means for each check deposited $30,000 was taken in cash. Jeff wrote paychecks for himself and a woman called Maria Garcia. He paid the utilities for the first month but was in arrears for the last three. The gas and electricity were cut off last week. The owner of the building was planning on evicting him since he paid the first and last months' rent when he first came, but nothing since."

Monica did some quick arithmetic and said, "If he took $30,000 in cash from each of the deposits, that would be $150,000. He put into the bank account about $75,000 which makes a total of $225.000 that he got from Mrs. Harkenstone. I thought maybe it was about $180,000. He must have told her they were going to stay in very fancy hotels. What about the rest of the $75,000 after the Paychecks for him and his secretary were cashed?" She licked the frosting off her fork as she contemplated the money.

"Another interesting wrinkle," continued Rick, "there were four large checks made out to a Southwest Consulting Firm for a total of $72,450.63. We haven't been able to locate that firm. Since all those checks have been cashed, the agency's account is currently down to $610.00."

"No checks made out to an airline, hotel, cruise ship etc. He did cheat Mrs. Harkenstone!" Monica felt a heaviness in her chest. "Gullible Mrs. Harkenstone will be shattered. Are you going to tell her?"

"That's a part of my job I hate. After this pleasant chat, I'm going down to the Church of the Sun and Moon and tell her the bad news." He sighed and took a sip of his coffee. "There's little chance of her recovering any of the money unless we get a real break. Who knows? He could have put it in an old sock."

"What about that comment of Sheila's he might have put money in a storage unit? She called a lot of them and didn't get anywhere, but she has a mysterious key. You remember the key in the Gideon Bible?" Monica's mind was dancing around as she sipped her coffee.

"The mysterious key in the Bible. It almost sounds like a title of a book," chuckled Rick. "We have a few angles to investigate. We're also trying to find his secretary, Maria Garcia. She was paid two weeks ago according to the date on the check."

"Have you talked to that insurance guy about the secretary? He might have seen her at some time or other." Monica stopped herself and blushed. "Of course, you have. I was just thinking aloud."

"Yes, Miss Marple, we talked to him." Rick chuckled again, but it was a kindly indulgent chuckle. " He said she was good looking and wore short skirts, but she wasn't around much. He spoke to her briefly about a month ago, but she needed to get to the post office in a hurry so she cut the conversation short. He said he could identify her if we had any pictures. In this city, there are many Hispanic women so we need more information."

"What about a computer? Every business has to have one," commented Monica as she tried to think like a detective.

"We didn't find one. I would guess he had a laptop which was stolen by the burglar. It probably contains encrypted information about the money and about his scam. Some one knows more than he or she is telling me," mused Rick as he looked at Monica with a serious expression on his face.

"What about this Southwest Consulting Firm?" asked Monica while she was trying to figure out how this new company fitted into the racket.

"Usually the crook makes up a phony company so he can launder his money. I imagine we'll find out Jeff used an alias on the Southwest Consulting Firm's checking account and paid himself through this bogus company. It takes a little while to set up the company with stationary, an address, etc. but it's been done before." Rick stretched out a leg while he explained the complexities of working a con game.

"John Spenser doesn't believe Jeff was a criminal, and now Sheila feels the same way. Mrs. Harkenstone trusted him absolutely. How could he fool these people?" Monica spoke aloud her questions about the gullibility of people.

Rick looked at her and said, "Remember your Shakespeare."

"Yes, of course, I remember several times the bard mentioned that type of behavior. The conspirators fooled Julius Caesar by pretending to be his friends while intending to kill him. Brutus told the men to hide their murderous intent 'in smiles and affability.' And in *Macbeth* Shakespeare says there are 'daggers in men's smiles.' I guess Shakespeare is right. If you appear to be good, people believe you."

Rick said, "It's like the scene between Antony and Cassius at the end of the play *Julius Caesar* when Antony accuses Cassius and the other conspirators of their vile deception. Anthony says, 'You showed your teeth like apes, and fawned like hounds/ And bowed like bondsmen, kissing Caesar's feet/ Whilst damned Casca, like a cur, behind/ Struck Caesar on the neck.'" When he finished, Rick had a pleased expression on his face. He shook his head and added, "I haven't thought of those lines for years, but they just came out."

"I'm impressed. When did you read *Julius Caesar?*" asked Monica as she radiated pure delight towards Rick.

"I played Antony in my high school play. The funeral oration took awhile to memorize, but I really liked saying it. Most of my friends wanted to be conspirators because they got to be in the play, but they didn't have to learn many lines, with the exception of Cassius, of course."

Monica and Rick beamed at each other while they remembered the play. Rick was the first to break the reverie. "I can't put off seeing Mrs. Harkenstone any longer. I have to be the messenger, and you know, of course, people's reaction to the bad news messenger."

"Yes, kill him. Bad news does spill over and includes who said it. I'm sorry you have to be in that position. I really like Mrs. Harkenstone. She's sort of crazy but in a kind way. Imagine using your own money to finance a trip for 20 people." Monica felt sympathy for Rick who at that moment had a sag to his shoulders. She suddenly had an inspiration. "Would it help if I went with you?" she asked.

"Really, would you do that?" Rick brightened. His entire face had a hopeful cast as he regarded Monica.

She stood up and said, "Let's go. I don't know what I can say to lighten your task, but I'll go with you." Rick took her arm and the two went out to tackle together the repugnant duty of informing a nice lady she had been deceived by a charming young man.

14

Mrs. Harkenstone was in her Moon Goddess gown when Monica and Rick met her in the Moon Room. Rick had phoned ahead so she was expecting them. She walked toward them extending her hand. "Detective Miller and Miss Walters, how nice to see you again."

"I'm sorry I'm the one who has to bring you some hurtful information," said Rick as soon as they were seated. He cleared his throat, fidgeted in his chair, gave a tug to his collar, and blurted out, "The Moonbeam Travel Agency didn't make any payments to any hotels in Egypt, any airlines, or any tours. I'm afraid you're a victim of a swindle."

The Moon Goddess stared at him for a moment and snapped, "Detective Miller, how dare you tell me that! I have receipts from the Moonbeam Travel Agency. That nice young man would never do anything wrong. You are mistaken."

"I'm sorry, ma'am, but the receipts only indicate you paid the travel agency. The receipts don't mean anyone else was paid," Rick explained.

"Of course, they were paid. Jeff told me we had electronic tickets for the airline and the hotels," the Moon Goddess argued. She pursed her lips and shot him a baleful look. Her back stiffened, and she crossed her arms over her chest.

Monica leaned towards her and said softly, "I know this is a shock to hear, but the police will try to get back your money just as soon as possible."

"Young lady, I haven't lost any money. Are you, also, saying Jeff was a crook? How dare you speak ill of the dead. Good-bye." She rose from her chair and pointed at the door.

"I think she just kicked us out of the church," murmured Monica to Rick under her breath as they sidled out of the room. "Maybe Jeff was like a son to her, and she just can't bear the thought of a betrayal."

Rick nodded. "It's sad. I've know some hustlers in my day, and they can be very honest looking and friendly."

After they climbed down the stairs, they saw Star munching on a pepperoni, cheese, and sausage pizza in the Pallas Pizza room. When Rick told him the news, he didn't argue; he believed it. He crammed a big piece of pizza in his mouth and chewed on it while he digested the bad news. He moaned, "This is terrible, just terrible! I was looking forward to this trip. What are we going to do? This is awful."

Monica repeated, "The police are trying to find the money. Maybe you'll be able to still go on your trip." After she said that, she wondered why Rick wasn't supporting her statement. He just gave Star the facts, nothing more.

Star almost started to cry as he thought of all the good things he was going to miss. " I wanted to see the museum of Ra. The Moon Goddess and I were going First Class on the airline. I"ve never flown First Class, and I hear you get a glass of champagne as soon as you sit down. This is terrible. I bought new clothes for the trip."

In the midst of his misery, Star ordered another pizza. Monica wanted to leave, but she waited for Rick to make the decision. Rick repeated the facts and didn't give Star any hope for reimbursement. After several minutes, he concluded their visit by saying, "I'll let you know when we have more information. Feel free to call me."

Star mumbled, "Yes, let me know. This is terrible." He finished the last of the pizza and looked at the counter to see if the new one was ready yet. He didn't seem to care that the messengers of bad news were leaving.

As Monica and Rick walked back to the car, he said, "Thanks for going with me. It's hard to see people suffer."

Monica changed the mood by joking, "If Star keeps eating pizza, he's not going to fit into his new clothes. He'll have to wears his sun robes outside the church."

They made light hearted conversation as they rode back to the Moonbeam Travel Agency where Monica had left her car. When he pulled up to the curb, Monica saw Sheila and the dogs standing outside the door of the insurance agency.

Dressed in jeans and a tight, black tee shirt, Sheila was talking to the insurance agent while the dogs twisted their leashes around her ankles.

"Hi," she shouted, "I've been waiting for you, Monica."

Rick turned to Monica. "Looks like you have someone who wants to see you, and I have work to do. I'll see you later." He waved and strode off to talk to the uniformed policeman who was standing at the door of the travel agency.

Sheila rushed over to Monica. The dogs wagged their tails as they ran over to Monica who bent down to pet them. Their little tongues gave her a couple slurps before she could get out of range.

Breathlessly Sheila asked, "Will you help me out? It shouldn't take very long, but you know Albuquerque, and I really don't know the city that well even though we lived here for a few months. I have a puzzle, sort of a game, sort of a scavenger hunt."

Monica asked, "What do you mean?"

Sheila confessed, "I sort of borrowed Jeff's computer, the one he used for the peace movement. I used boobsandwhistles for the password, and I found a message for me from Jeff. He wrote I was the only woman he ever loved, and if something happened to him, he wanted me to have his money. He said he was under scrutiny and might have to leave quickly since he feared for his life. He didn't want to write exactly where the money was in case a stranger opened the file so he only wrote a clue. You know, just like in *The Da Vinci Code,* which was his favorite book."

"You need to tell Detective Miller," insisted Monica.

"Why does he have to know?" Sheila's mouth went into a pout.

"For one thing, that paper could shift the victim from John Spenser to Jeff." Monica put her hand on Sheila's arm. "It might even be dangerous for you."

"I'm not scared. Honestly, Monica, you're being overly dramatic," huffed Sheila.

"I'll try to help, but I can't promise you I won't tell Detective Miller. Jeff cheated someone out of a lot of money so if the money is found, he needs to know." Monica wanted to be honest with Sheila, even if it meant she wouldn't be privy to an important part of the investigation.

"Wouldn't you like to be on the inside track and find the money before the police do?" Sheila taunted.

Monica thought Sheila couldn't have picked a better way to get her to help. The idea that she could be ahead of the police in solving a crime was heady indeed. "Well, okay, I promise I won't tell Detective Miller until we find the money."

Sheila thrust a piece of paper into Monica's hand.

The paper said, "Mother Earth keeps what you want,/ But you must find the stone of Arthur./ First look for the church like an eagle that faces west./ More will await you there."

"The church sounds like it's Native American, but I don't know of any in Albuquerque." Monica quizzically looked at Sheila who was looking at the dogs.

"It didn't make any sense to me at all," said Sheila. "I've been working on this clue for hours."

"The church like an eagle could be St. Paul's Lutheran because it's always looked like a bird to me. The one sharp corner looks like a beak, and a window on each side could be eyes. It doesn't have wings, but the eagle could be sitting." Monica enjoyed puzzles so trying to crack this clue was fun. She bit her lower lip as she concentrated on the architecture of St. Paul's Lutheran Church.

"Let's go. That church could be the one." Sheila swung into action. She opened the back door of her car for the dogs and indicated to Monica she should hop in the front passenger seat. "Give me the directions," she ordered

When they arrived at the church, the sun was setting. As they analyzed the outside appearance to see if it fit the clue, a ray of sun hit the windows which indeed glowed like eyes. Sheila shouted, "I think you're right." She pulled the car into the empty parking lot and jumped out while making sure that the dogs stayed in. Monica closed her door carefully too.

"We need to find stones," shouted Sheila as she darted around the landscaped areas that had small shrubs and bushes in decorative places. Because of the fading light, she bent over to see better.

Monica had a hard time keeping up with the bustling Sheila. After tromping around the front, they branched out and checked little pockets of greenery on the sides of the church. At the back, they discovered a rock garden with little plants artistically stuck here and there. Monica theorized about the clue to Sheila. "You know 'Arthur's stone' could refer to the rock used as a test for the future king. According to the story, whoever could remove the sword that was stuck in the rock would be King; however, I hardly think we'll find a sword out here in this little garden or anyplace in Albuquerque," she added.

"Could Jeff have meant something else?" asked Sheila.

As they walked through the little garden, Sheila noticed some of the rocks were painted in bright colors and had little crude designs on them. "Look, Monica, aren't they cute? I bet some nursery school teacher let the kids paint rocks. Here's one that says, 'God's rock' and another that says, 'I lov you.'"

"And here's one that says 'Arthur's stone.'" shouted Monica in triumph. "We need to look in the earth." Quickly she lifted up the stone, dug a little with her hand, and found a folded piece of paper in the dirt. Sheila dived for the paper and with trembling fingers shook off the soil and unfolded the tiny scrap.

"It's another clue," she said.

Monica peered over her shoulder, and they both eagerly read, "Old here, but not old everywhere,/ Walk in the square and see the circle,/ Mother Nature's secret place under the flowers with the faces."

"What is it? Have you figured it out, Monica?" Sheila hoped for instant recognition of the place.

"It's tricky. There are many places that are old. We here in Albuquerque think our churches and forts are old, but when I went to Europe, their churches and stuff are centuries older. The oldest church is in Old Town which is the historical district." Monica was pondering out loud. She reread the next line about the square and the circle. "There's a town square in the middle of Old Town."

"That's it!" shrieked Sheila. "The town square has a round gazebo in the middle. I remember because one day when I was there shopping for jewelry, a mariachi group was playing in the gazebo. There were pansies planted in a circle. Now the clue makes sense."

"I think so, too. Let's check it out," Monica said, and they ran back to the car. While they were fastening their seat belts, a green van drove into the parking lot and stopped. Neither of them paid much attention to the other car as they exited and headed west; however, when Sheila turned south, she briefly saw a green van in her back mirror. Several blocks later, when she made another turn, she saw the same van.

"Monica, remember that green van that drove into the parking space. Look in the mirror. Do you see it?" Sheila's hands tightened on the steering wheel.

"Yes, I see it. Do you suppose someone is tailing us?"

"I've never been tailed before,"said Sheila.

"I've never been tailed before either. From what I'm seen on TV, you should drive fast and make unexpected turns to fool your pursuer," advised Monica as she kept shifting her eyes from one mirror to another. At the next light, Sheila went through the yellow. The green van didn't stop but went through on the red.

Several horns blared out, and one driver even opened his window and shouted some obscenity

Sheila turned east at the next corner, drove south, turned west, and north. The green van followed. "Do you have any ideas?"

"Confuse him," answered Monica in a determined voice.

Sheila kept turning corners and making circles until she got tired of driving. On an impulse she slipped into the parking lot of the Erna Ferguson Library. "Let's see if he comes in, and maybe he'll get close enough so we can identify him?"

They waited quietly. The dogs jumped around in the back seat but didn't bark. Monica held her breath and hoped she'd get at least a glimpse of the driver. They waited for five, ten, fifteen minutes and nothing.

"Someone thinks you know where the money is. That's the only reason why someone would follow us. Are you sure I'm the only one you told about the message from Jeff?" asked Monica.

Sheila didn't even ponder the question. "I didn't tell anyone, except you, but Larry and John are suspicious. They think I'm holding back information on the money. I bet one of them is following me. Let's go back to the hotel for tonight. Tomorrow I'll walk over there with the dogs since Old Town isn't far from the hotel. When the sun is shining, I can see if one of them is following me easily."

Monica craned her neck to look from side to side as she hoped the green van would make an appearance. "Whoever is tailing us should have chosen a car that blends in with the usual traffic. In Albuquerque, most of the cars are white or silver. A green car stands out."

"You're right. I don't think either Larry or John has much experience in tailing anyone. I'm surprised whoever it is could keep up with me. I did some pretty good driving. I can outfox either one of them," Sheila boasted.

They chatted about ten minutes before Sheila pulled out of the library parking lot and headed back to her hotel. No green van was in sight. Each of the women kept looking, however, for the sudden appearance of the suspicious car.

"Will you call me after you get the clue in the pansy bed? I really want to know what's going on." Monica wrote her cell phone number on a piece of paper and stuck it on top of the dashboard. "You can call me anytime, even if I'm at school. I'll excuse myself and go out into the hall to talk."

"Sure, I'll call you. I'm going to have breakfast outside and linger over my coffee. If I don't see either one of those conniving rats, I'll amble over to Old Town. I'll play it cool. I hope Jeff isn't going to drag out these clues like Dan Brown did. And don't worry, Monica, we'll both go to the police."

Monica left Sheila's car and got into her own. As she drove home, she wondered if Sheila really would call her.

15

All day long Monica waited for a call from Sheila. Her phone didn't ring once. Monica started to worry Sheila had found another written clue in the pansy bed, deciphered it herself, went to the treasure trove, took the money, and skipped town. On the other hand, she had promised to tell the police. Monica went back and forth about what could have happened. It was after 4:00 when she got the call.

"It's Sheila. This morning I sat outside and talked with Larry and John. John told me about the design for tee shirts he's preparing for the Church of the Sun and Moon. He said Jeff's reputation will be restored after the police find all the paid reservations etc. Larry didn't say much. He just acted nervous as always and told me both John and Jeff owed him money. Same old, same old, blah, blah."

"I'm not surprised. I've heard them say the same things. But you didn't tell me if you found a note in the pansy bed," said Monica who doodled on a piece of scrap paper while she talked on the phone.

"After awhile John and Larry left to eat lunch at some Mexican restaurant on Central Avenue. They asked me to go along, but I begged off. After I saw their car leave, I walked with the dogs over to Old Town since it's only two blocks from the hotel."

Sheila took a deep breath and continued, "A lot of tourists were milling around so no one paid any attention to what I was doing. I went directly to the gazebo in the middle of the plaza. Some of the dirt around the pansy bed looked like it had been scuffed up. I bent down and felt around. The dogs got interested and started to dig. And bless their little hearts, they found it. I snatched the folded piece of paper quickly, looked around, and casually kept walking, just as if I was going to do some shopping."

"What did it say? I'm dying to find out."

"I'll read it to you, if you're sure your phone hasn't been tapped," said Sheila in a hesitant voice.

"Who would want to tap my phone? I'm sure you can talk freely," answered Monica as she drew a big ear and stick figure holding a phone on her scrap paper.

"Here's the clue: "Look high but not low,/ Money matters especially when you're hungry,/ Mother Nature always knows,/ Under the glorified one,/ That flaps, waves, but never falls." Sheila read the description of the new hiding place in a whisper.

Monica let the clue roll around in her head for awhile, but nothing emerged. "I'll have to think it over. This is a tough one."

"Do you think he's referring to a bird in that last line? A bird sanctuary maybe?" Sheila mused.

"No, because the riddle said 'under the glorified one that flaps' which doesn't refer to a bird. Sometimes our flag is called old glory. The Mother Nature line probably means he put it in the dirt, and you'll have to dig it out. So far all of them have been hidden that way.

But the reference to money has me confused," said Monica. She bit her Bic pen while she thought. "The restaurant on Sandia Peak is called High Finance. That could be it."

"You're right. All the clues support that idea: high, hungry, money. I've been there once; in fact it was with Jeff. There's a tall flag pole next to the restaurant that flies the good old red, white, and blue. Let's go there now," said Sheila in an excited voice.

"It'll take an hour to get there, and by that time it'll be too dark to see anything. I'll go with you tomorrow after school," replied Monica who didn't want to stumble around with a flashlight looking for a clue on top of the mountain tonight.

"I want to find out as soon as I can. I may go without you. Otherwise I'll call you tomorrow," said Sheila who hung up abruptly.

Monica sighed and thought Sheila probably would go by herself.

Almost a minute later, the phone rang again. "This is Rick Miller."

"Hello, Rick, how are you?" Thrilled to hear his voice, Monica's lips turned up in a smile.

"I know I'm calling late, but I just read in the paper that The Bare Bear's Theater is putting on a new version of *Hamlet*. They're sold out all week except for tonight. Are you interested?"

"Yes, I'd love to go. I've seen several versions of the play, and it's always intriguing to see a production in a new setting. I haven't hear of The Bare Bear's Theater. Where is it?" While she was talking, she felt her heart skip a beat.

"It's a little place on Fourth Street. You know how all these small theater groups find an empty warehouse or whatever and put on a show. This theater is in a small building with perhaps 80 or 90 seats. The audience and the actors consist mainly of college theater majors who have lots of enthusiasm. You'll never believe it, but the setting for *Hamlet* is a circus. King Claudius takes over ownership of the circus after the death of his brother. He marries his brother's wife, Gertie, who is the lead performer on the trapeze. Hamlet, her son, is the lion tamer. Crazy, isn't it?"

Monica laughed, "This show is going to be a riot. Thank you for inviting me."

"I'll pick you up at 7:00. See you then."

A little before 7:00, he rang the bell. Wearing a green sweater set with a green striped scarf, Monica opened the door. She felt rather giddy when she looked into those marvelous soft brown eyes. Mitsey trotted over, sniffed his hand, and wagged her tail. He patted the dog's head and said, "Good girl." Monica and the dog were both pleased.

"You look lovely tonight," he stammered.

"Thank you, " she murmured. After a short pause, he helped her with her jacket. She gave a final pat to Mitsey, and they left. As they drove, they talked about the case briefly, but mostly they made small talk.

The Bare Bear's Theater was "off Broadway" in more ways than one. It was literally one street from Broadway Avenue and did experimental theater. Previously, it had been a Dairy Queen located between a tire repair store on one side and an organic food store on the other. A large poster tacked on the door showed Hamlet facing a snarling lion with a whip in one hand and in the other hand a chair, legs straight out in a defensive position.

After they were seated, Monica noticed most of the audience consisted of college students and their young friends. All the 80 or 90 seats were filled, and a couple people stood in the back.

The set design was the interior of the big top with gravel on the floor, a center ring, and bleachers on the side. In the first act, the director used strobe lights to flicker on the ghost who wasn't dressed in armor but in a plaid shirt as the previous owner of the circus. The lines referring to the armor were left out.

When Marcellus said, "Something is rotten in the state of the circus," Monica thought the line lacked the serious, ominous tone of the original. Monica looked at Rick when that line was spoken, and they both chuckled.

Although Monica knew she shouldn't talk during the performance, she whispered, "I like Papa Polonius's advice to his son, Laertes. And my favorite line of his advice is 'To thine own self be true.'" Rick nodded in agreement. She added, "When I teach the play, the students really remember it."

"Hamlet's line, 'That one may smile, and smile, and be a villain' fits what we've talked about before that a friendly face can hide a criminal mind," he whispered back.

When Hamlet gave his "To be, or not to be" speech, he looked out a tent flap at the elephants. This was done by projecting a movie of elephants milling around a water hole while using their trunks to splash water on their backs. Monica thought the seriousness of contemplating life and death was lost by watching happy elephants talking a bath. She poked Rick in the side during the speech and bit her lip to keep from snorting.

During the intermission after Act III, they dawdled in the reception area . The chatter among the audience members indicated the students liked the new setting. "So relevant" and "So now" were the most often used phrases. Monica and Rick didn't praise the adaptation, but rather they got a kick out of the new setting.

In Act IV, the director used the same technology as before to change Ophelia's death scene by projecting a movie that showed pacing, growling tigers. Ophelia approached the tigers' cage and sang her little song. When she walked off stage, it appeared she entered the cage. The next movie clip showed the tigers in a feeding frenzy. Instead of falling into the stream and drowning, she became dinner for a pair of hungry tigers.

Hamlet's death scene was also changed, but not as dramatically. In the last act, the sword duel between Hamlet and Laertes became a dagger fight. The weapons were provided by the knife thrower, Horatio. During the duel, the other circus members ate popcorn and drank lemonade. Gertrude drank the poisoned lemonade that was supposed to be for Hamlet.

"That last scene reminds me of Jeff Landsdon's death. He drank the poison that was meant for John," Monica commented after the curtain came down, and the actors had taken their bows to an enthusiastic audience.

"I'm not so sure the poison was intended to kill John," answered Rick. "But I won't say anything more about that just yet. But what did you think of Hamlet as a philosophical lion tamer?"

"A little weird. I prefer a more traditional rendition, but some would say this production was 'cutting edge,'" said Monica, "but I'm so glad I saw it. The students loved it. Did you see how they swarmed over to talk to the director?"

As they walked to the car, Rick asked, "Have you seen Sheila lately?"

Monica's conscience gave her a tug. "Yes, I saw her yesterday, and I promised I wouldn't tell you something she's going to tell you after she finds something that she found out about in a mysterious way that I don't know," rambled Monica in a long run-on sentence.

Rick chuckled, "I always like an uncomplicated answer. I'll be glad to hear what she is going to tell me after she finds something you promised you couldn't tell me. What could be clearer?" He was still chortling.

"I really want to tell you, really I do. But if I tell, after I promised I wouldn't tell, then I would be dishonest, and she won't take me on the next clue finding mission. I'll call her tomorrow and ask to be released from my promise," Monica said as she tried to salvage both her integrity and her relationship with Rick.

He drove her home, walked her to the door, and hesitated. She looked at him and purred, "Thank you for a lovely evening." She wondered if she should look at him or if that would be too bold, almost asking for a kiss. Instead she put the key in the lock. "Good night, Rick."

He gave her a warm smile and also said, "Good night."

She had hardly greeted Mitsey when the phone rang. Cradling the phone on her shoulder while she fed Mitsey a dog biscuit, she said, "Hello."

"This is Sheila. I found another clue. I drove up the mountain to the top of Sandia Peak where the High Finance Restaurant is. While I was driving up there, I kept looking for a green van, but I didn't see one. A gray Prius, just like the one John rented, came up the mountain road several cars behind mine. I was very clever and pretended I was going to eat in the restaurant. I went in and walked to the restroom. A few minutes later, I slipped back out. The gray Prius wasn't parked in the lot so perhaps it had gone some place else. Anyway, I felt free to poke around in the dirt at the base of the flag pole. I used a stick to dig in a soft spot where I found a folded piece of paper about an inch deep in the soil. Another riddle."

"That's great, Sheila. What's the new clue?" asked Monica while she twisted her body to take off her jacket and not drop the phone that was still clenched between her chin and shoulder.

"Here it is. 'A pot of gold is what you want/ You know where I went before/ Don't take the simple way/ Truth is always the best answer/ Take my age and double it.'"

"You told me he hid money in a dresser in a storage unit before. I suppose he's referring to that place," said Monica immediately.

"Yes, I think so, too. I've always thought he had a pile of money in storage, and it's all mine! I'm so excited," chirped Sheila.

"Was his age 34?" Monica suddenly remembered what she had found on the day that Jeff died.

"Yes, how did you know?"

"I just thought of a number I found on a slip of paper in Jeff's room. The number was 68. I almost forgot about it until I heard the last line of the clue." Monica couldn't believe she had forgotten about the tiny piece of paper she had unfolded with so much difficulty. That piece of the puzzle fell nicely into the clue. "It's the number of a storage unit, isn't it?"

"But which one? I'm going to check the telephone book and read through their list. Thanks a lot for your help, Monica."

"I'll read through the list too. If I get an idea, I'll let you know. Now can we tell Rick tomorrow?" pleaded Monica as she pulled out her telephone book.

Sheila paused before she said, "Well, tomorrow should be okay. But don't say anything until I call. Then we'll go together."

After Monica had put down the phone, she thought Sheila now had the number and key to some storage unit. It shouldn't take too long to find it, and maybe the money could be returned. But what about the killer? She still didn't know. She, also, didn't know who was the intended victim.

Monica looked at the list of storage units and picked out three that had possibilities: Shamrock, Rainbow, and Honest Abe. The Rainbow appeared to be the perfect answer for the pot of gold, but it could be too simple. Honest Abe may be the one.

She thought about calling Sheila but decided she'd wait until tomorrow. She was tired and didn't want to think any more about burglary, murder, or hidden money.

Instead she thought about her evening with a fellow lover of Shakespeare. As she fed Mitsey another milk bone and scratched behind her ears, she pictured in her mind a human face with soft brown eyes. She didn't want to hold back any information for fear it could jeopardize this very special relationship.

16

During the entire teaching day, Monica kept thinking about the latest clue. Since all Sheila had to do was check a few storage units, Monica felt she should have received a report. If she didn't get a call in the next hour, she was going to tell Rick anyway. Rick expected to hear from her, and she didn't want to disappoint him. They had such a good time last night. Sheila should have told Rick everything by now because the storage unit could hold the answer to many questions.

Monica tried calling Sheila on her cell phone, but there was no answer. Since Monica was getting antsy and irritable just sitting at her desk, she decided to run over to the Barclay Towers. Monica mumbled to herself, "If I can't find Sheila at the hotel, I'll call Rick at once and have a clear conscience."

After arriving at the Barclay Towers a little after 4:00, she meandered through the outdoor table area, the lobby, and even the restrooms. After calling Sheila's cell phone three times, she headed for the desk to see if she was still registered when two dogs in pink sweaters came into view. Sheila had arrived.

" I've been looking for you everywhere. Did you find the storage unit?" Monica asked as she walked over to her. Stephanie pawed the air so Monica would pet her. Rhonda followed what the slightly older dog did and, also, sat and lifted her tiny paws. Monica couldn't resist a furry face and bent down to touch their little heads.

"Hi Monica, I've been busy packing and other things. I'm going to leave tomorrow," Sheila said while heading for the elevators and dragging the dogs with her.

Monica couldn't believe she was getting the cold shoulder. She stumbled after her while repeating the important question, "Did you find the storage unit?"

"Ah–No, no, I didn't." Sheila was talking over her shoulder at the same time she was punching the elevator button.

"We should tell the police about your clues," pressed Monica who couldn't understand Sheila's strange behavior. Yesterday, she had wanted her help and was friendly. Now, she was evasive, cold, and just plain weird. The dogs dancing around Monica's feet looked cute in their little pink sweaters, like little sausages. In fact they seemed much chubbier than before. They probably had eaten a lot of scraps while staying at the hotel.

"Not yet, maybe we'll tell the police tomorrow. Sorry, but I'm tired, and I'm going to lie down. I'll talk to you tomorrow." Sheila hit the elevator button again.

"I'm going to tell Rick. You said we'd tell the police today. Since you aren't going to, I feel I should," declared Monica in a determined voice.

"Whatever," replied Sheila as she and the dogs walked into the elevator that finally had come down to the lobby floor. The elevator door closed and whisked them away.

Monica took her cell phone out of her purse and punched in Rick's number. He answered on the second ring, and Monica babbled, "I can tell you now what I've been doing with Sheila who got a message from Jeff that had clues about where the money is hidden." She was almost out of breath as she let all the words gush out.

"I'm very interested. Let's meet at the Barclay Towers and sit in the sunshine at the outdoor tables. I'm ready for a break," said Rick. "I want to hear all the Sheila news. I need some fresh clues since I keep going over the same territory."

In less than 30 minutes, Monica and Rick were seated at an umbrella table. Rick crossed his legs and looked relaxed while Monica sat on the edge of her chair. In her haste to tell her news, she didn't even greet him, she just burst out, "Sheila got a message from Jeff that gave her clues to a supposed pot of money. I helped her figure out the clues. The last one indicated she should go to a storage unit."

"Whoa, let's take this a little slower. How did she get the message from Jeff? Did he relay it from above through a psychic?" Rick spoke facetiously, but it was an important question.

"It was a message in a computer Sheila 'borrowed.' Do you remember Sheila left the dogs in John's suite for one night. That was the night Jeff's laptop was stolen. We all thought it was funny the dogs didn't bark when the intruder entered. They didn't bark because they knew the intruder, Sheila. She took the laptop for a day and later returned it after she found the clue. She guessed a password that opened a file Jeff had written for her. When we were talking one day, she said he used to call her 'boobs and whistles.' I bet that was the password for his encrypted computer file." Monica's eyes gleamed as she put her ideas together.

Monica expected Rick would show a little enthusiasm, but he didn't even open his eyes wide. He just sat there relaxed, stroked his chin, and cleared his throat while she babbled with excitement.

"Jeff really called her 'boobs and whistles'? We had that laptop for almost a week, and the boys didn't think of that password. I never would have guessed it either," said Rick as he shook his head. At that point, the waitress served up two plates of chocolate cake with vanilla ice cream covered with hot fudge sauce. As Monica looked at the delicious dessert, she was glad that she was one of those lucky people who didn't gain weight.

After taking a bite, she continued with her story, "When Sheila returned the laptop, she put it in the closet so everyone would think John had misplaced it. I didn't see the message, but according to her, Jeff said he felt his life was threatened. He wanted her to get the 'pot of gold' because she was the only woman he ever really loved. The first clue lead us to a rock in the landscaped area of St. Paul's Lutheran Church."

"A rock by the church? Some say the church is built on a rock," joked Rick, "but tell me more."

"Under the rock we dug up a piece of paper that had a few lines about a circle in a square in an old place where there were flowers with faces. We decided the note was referring to the central plaza which is in the shape of a square in the historic area of Old Town. The circle was the gazebo which has a bed of pansies around it. However, we didn't go there because we were being followed. So we went home instead."

"Followed? How did you know?" inquired Rick

"We kept seeing this bright green van. Imagine tailing someone in a green car in Albuquerque. Sheila went around in circles, but the van stayed with us. We couldn't see the driver." Monica slowed down to eat another bite of chocolate cake.

"Monica, you could be in some danger. I want you to call me if there's some place you want to go with Sheila," said Rick in a serious tone. "Whoever this person is who was tailing you might harm you."

"Really? Sheila thought it was John who wanted to keep tabs on her in case she found Jeff's money. She thinks he's kind of a wimp. According to her, he doesn't do anything if he might get his shirt sweaty or muss his hair."

"The person who followed you might not be a wimp. You need to be careful," cautioned Rick.

"I'll be careful. But I have more to tell you. There are more clues just like in *The Da Vinci Code*. Sheila went on her own to Old Town and found another folded piece of paper in the pansy bed. She called me to decipher the clue. It was about money, hunger, and high places which I figured out was the High Finance

Restaurant on top of Sandia peak." Monica had slowed down in telling her story in order to keep slurping up the ice cream with chocolate sauce.

"This fellow was rather clever. You could have called me since I like to figure out puzzles," said Rick who was spooning his ice cream.

"I promised her I wouldn't tell you until we found the unit. Then she was going to go with me to reveal all of this. When I saw her this afternoon, I said I had to tell you today. I feel I have been honorable."

"Yes, you have been honorable, and I appreciate your integrity. But I want to know the final clue."

" I memorized it. 'A pot of gold is what you want/ You know where I went before/ Don't take the simple way/ Truth is always the best answer/ Take my age and double it.' Sheila told me he had squirreled away money before in a dresser in a storage unit because he didn't want any record of the money. When I checked the names of the storage units, there were three that could fit: Shamrock, Rainbow, and Honest Abe."

"I guess the Honest Abe Storage," said Rick while he licked the last bit of chocolate off his spoon.

"Me, too," said Monica. "Since his age is 34, the storage unit should be 68."

"Sounds good. I need to talk with her."

Before Rick took out his cell phone, Monica looked to the left and saw Randy coming toward them. Randy waved and then walked over to the table. She looked at Rick and asked, "Have you caught the killer yet?"

Before she heard an answer, she sat down next to him as if you wanted to chat about the police's efforts. She was dressed in a sky blue suit with a black lace blouse. When she put her hands on the table, Monica noticed she had been to a manicurist since each bright red nail had a little moon on the top. As a passing fancy, Monica thought the Goddess of the Moon might like to know the name of the shop.

"No, not yet. We have a few ideas," he said as he pushed his empty dish away.

"John and I believe this kook is long gone from here; however, John is worried this killer may try another attempt in Atlanta where we'll be going soon. Could you alert the authorities there so he could feel he is somewhat protected?" Randy quickly glanced at her watch as she finished speaking.

"I don't know if that will be necessary, but we can talk more about his fear later on. Where is he now?" asked Rick.

"I'm going to meet him any minute. We have business to discuss." She peeked at her watch again and looked around. "There he is. I see him by the door. See you later." Randy popped up and trotted over to the door where John stood smoothing back his hair.

A man walked over to their table just after Randy left. Monica recognized him as the insurance salesman in the office next to the Moonbeam Travel Agency. He shook hands with Rick and said, "Burt Rider, Homeland Insurance."

"Yes, Mr. Rider, how's it going?" replied Rick.

"Good, good. I see it didn't take you long to find Maria Garcia. I'm impressed," said Burt as he watched Randy disappear in the hotel.

"What do you mean?" Rick wrinkled his forehead. Monica ,also, was perplexed.

"You were just talking to her," Burt explained as he looked from one startled face to another.

"Are you sure that lady in the light blue suit was Maria Garcia?" asked Rick. "She's not Hispanic."

"I never said she was Hispanic. Sure, she's the one who worked for the Moonbeam Travel Agency. I talked to her a couple times. I was even going to ask her for a date, but she always had to hurry away," Burt said confidently.

Rick jumped up with his cell phone in his hand. As he left the table, he said quietly to Monica, "I have to leave now. I'll call you later. I have a few questions to ask Randy-Maria."

Burt had a puzzled look on his face when Rick abruptly departed. "What's the big deal?"

Monica sat there stunned. "It is a big deal. It means Randy, acting as Maria, helped Jeff swindle Mrs. Harkenstone!"

17

Burt blinked his eyes a couple times. "What swindle?"

Monica recovered enough from her astonishment to reply, "Jeff Landsdon took a lot of money from an old lady who believed he paid for airlines, hotels, lectures, guided tours. We think he hid the money in preparation for a quick exit; however, someone murdered him before he had the chance to leave town and disappear. Randy, as Maria Garcia, must have helped him since she worked there."

"Wow!" Burt paused as he processed this information. "She's really pretty, and I liked her. I liked Jeff, too, although I only spoke with him a couple times. They didn't look like crooks. They looked like regular, nice people. I felt kind of sorry for them because I never saw any clients go into the place."

"Frankly, I'm having a rough time believing she's involved in this shady business, too. When Sheila went on and on about hidden money, Randy didn't say a thing." Monica tried to put this new puzzle piece into some form. She kept her thoughts to herself as she wondered if the hoax and Jeff's murder were related.

Monica wanted action instead of just mulling over and over what could have happened. She decided to head for the storage unit. "Burt, I have to go, but your information was very helpful. I'll let you know what happens." While she walked to her car, she scrounged around in her purse for her cell phone. She called Leslie.

Leslie answered on the first ring. Monica, you've been running around with Sheila and haven't said a word to me about what you're been doing," sniffed Leslie. Her hurt tone came through to Monica who felt guilty about not keeping her best friend in the loop. "Sheila made me promise not to tell, but now I can. It's rather complicated, but here's what happened." Monica took a deep breath and told her about the series of clues.

After Monica related all the events, Leslie said, "Okay, I forgive you, but I still think you could have told me a little bit of what was going on." Her voice lost most of its wounded tone, but a trace of hurt feelings still remained.

"Let's go to Honest Abe Storage right now," Monica urged.

"Okay," Leslie said, "But you have a few problems. You don't know whose name Jeff used when he rented the unit. Also, you don't have a key."

"We'll figure all those things out when we get there. We can sit in the parking lot for awhile. Maybe the police are at the storage place already because Rick had his cell phone out when he took off. If he got Sheila's key, he could open the unit unless you need a judge to sign a search warrant. On *Law and Order* they're always getting search warrants." Monica sifted through all the possibilities.

Monica picked up Leslie at her apartment, looked up the address for Honest Abe in the telephone book, and drove across town to an isolated enclosure of buildings next to the railroad tracks. A high 10 foot fence surrounded a large building, parking lots, and about 80 storage units. Monica drove through the open gate and parked as close as she could to the front door of the main building. Two cars were parked beside hers in the front gravel parking lot, but Monica couldn't see how many cars were parked along the side of the large building because of all the cottonwood trees obscuring the area.

Since the sun was fading, the edges of the building and the trees blurred into a muddle of murky shadows. Along side the fence, vines grew tall with their scratchy tentacles poking out in all directions Monica saw overgrown, unkempt shrubs placed without design or pattern on blotchy spots of grass next to the front door. Some tree branches poked out at odd angles and appeared to be arms with long fingers just like in a Disney movie she had seen as a child. No welcoming outside lights, just dark shapes. "It's spooky out here," Monica squeaked as she turned off the car.

" That dark shape to the left of the building looks like a man hiding in the shadows. I also saw what looked like a green van parked in that side lot. Maybe we should just go home."

They sat still and watched the shadows. No man emerged. "We're just letting our imaginations take over. Nobody is there; we're just seeing funny tree shadows," said Monica.

"Maybe, but let's wait a little longer."

After five minutes, Monica got restless. "I want to do something. Let's ask the desk person if anyone has been asking about number 68. We'll go directly into the main building through the front door. Nothing could happen if we walk fast."

"Okay, I guess," said Leslie as she bit her lip.

They opened their car doors slowly, looked both ways as if they were going to cross a busy street, and scooted up to the door. Inside the building, a woman with her hair in big pink bristled curlers yawned behind a desk. "Need help?" she growled.

Monica cleared her throat, swallowed a couple times, and said, "Could you tell us if anyone has asked about number 68 in the last few days?"

"Huh? Got yourself a key for number 68?" the woman asked as her curlers bounced up and down. Her eyes kept straying to a small television set on the corner of a shelf.

"Well, no," admitted Monica, "but I would like to know if my friend came by earlier to check on a few things we have in the unit." Monica crossed her fingers as she told her fib and avoided looking at Leslie who remained standing at her side.

"You got no key, can't open," grunted the woman whose jowls quivered as she shook her head. The TV game show held her attention more than two keyless women.

"Has anyone been here and inquired about number 68?" persisted Monica.

"I donna know," the lady muttered. "That dog gal mabbe."

"The dog gal is probably Sheila. I thought she was holding something back when I saw her today. She practically raced for the elevator," whispered Monica to Leslie.

"When was she here?" Monica asked the desk woman who was now chewing on a Hershey bar while her eyes stayed riveted on the TV screen.

"Now," was the laconic reply

Monica looked out the window and saw two little dogs in pink sweaters bounding down the sidewalk with their blonde human mother right behind them. They apparently were coming from the storage units and were now heading for the parking lot directly in front of the building. Monica turned on her heel, bolted for the door, and shouted, "Sheila ."

Sheila stopped. "Hi, Monica, Leslie. Why are you here?"

"We came to find out what's in the storage unit," said Monica. "I figured out the riddle referred to Honest Abe, and I told that to Detective Miller. He'll probably be here soon. But Sheila, you're acting strange. Did you find the money?"

"Yes, I just now found it in the drawer of a chest. I don't know how much, but there's a lot of $100 bills in neat little piles in the top drawer. You caught me just as I was going to call you so we could go to the police together. Naturally, I wouldn't take any money until everything was legal. I'm not even carrying a purse." Sheila took her cell phone out of her pocket and held her arms away from her body to show she wasn't concealing any packets of money.

"I wasn't accusing you," apologized Monica. " I didn't think you'd take the money until it was legal."

Sheila sniffed, "You looked at me funny."

"Sorry." Monica lowered her head in humility.

"What's the phone number of that detective who keeps snooping around?" asked Sheila as she held out the phone ready to punch in the numbers.

After Monica gave her the number, Sheila called and reported the find. After she hung up, she said, "It'll take Detective Miller about 30 minutes to get here, but he said he'd send a regular patrol car that's in the vicinity to come, too."

As they waited, Monica could hardly contain her curiosity. "Let's go back there and look around. We shouldn't touch anything, but if we just look, there shouldn't be any problem."

Sheila shrugged her shoulders. "Sure, why not."

By now, the sun had gone down completely. Gloomy shadows covered the path, the buildings, and the cars. Monica sensed someone lurked near the storage units, but she didn't see anything. Gravel crunched under their feet as they hurried to number 68. The dogs pattered beside them. Monica heard a crackle of a twig off to the left. "What was that?" she whispered. They all stopped, but there were no more sounds.

"Probably a dog or a cat," answered Sheila. Her dogs' heads both pointed to the left, and their noses sniffed the air.

"We're almost at 68. Let's walk faster," urged Monica. Everyone quickened their pace while listening for any more ominous noises. When they finally arrived at their destination, Sheila took out the key, opened the door, and flipped on the light. The unit held a sofa, a couple swivel chairs, two rolled up carpets, and a chest of drawers.

"It wouldn't hurt if we just looked at the money. We won't count it, but just look. What do you say, Sheila?" asked Monica who had never seen a large stash or a small stash or even much money. Her checks went directly to the bank, and she usually took out $100 in twenties for cash purchases.

"Why not?" Sheila opened the top drawer so they could peek inside. Monica and Leslie bent over the drawer which held nice little stacks of $100 dollar bills enclosed by rubber bands.

"Wow!" All three women were so entranced by the money, they didn't hear shuffling noises until the dogs yapped. The barking brought them out of the spell. They turned towards the door and saw John holding a small gun.

"Hand it over!" he yelled. "Throw down your phones. Don't make a move!"

Although Monica was scared to death, she thought he wasn't making sense. While he was ordering them to throw down their phones, he, also, didn't want them to move. And he wanted someone to hand him the money. Since he was lurching a bit, Monica thought he might have had four or five martinis which could account for his mixed up commands. Monica, also, noticed he wasn't holding the gun steady. It kept moving in a circular way, but always in their direction.

A gun held by a shaky drunk scared the three women enough to drop their phones. Monica really wanted to bend down and set hers on the cement carefully, but she thought he might be trigger happy. When the phones made three sharp clunks as they hit the floor, Monica scrunched her shoulders and hoped hers survived. The dogs jumped and barked in their most ferocious way, but since each weighted about eight pounds, their protection value wasn't high.

Sheila was the first to recover from the shock of seeing John holding a gun. "For God's sake, John, why are you doing this? This is my money. I have his will." Narrowing her eyes, she strategically added, " Maybe I could let you have a little part of it."

Monica blurted out, "This money belongs to Mrs. Harkenstone!"

John shouted, "It's my money. I worked hard for it!"

"You worked hard for it? Hah! Jeff did the sting. You didn't know anything about it. When you heard about his scamming Mrs. Harkenstone, you sneaked around trying to find out where he put his loot. You've been following me and hoping I would lead you to it. You can't have it." Sheila announced.

"Sheila, I have a gun. It's mine!"

"It's mine," shouted Sheila disregarding his firearm.

"It's mine. I earned it!" bellowed John.

"Yeah, sure. You did nothing!" screeched Sheila as she jutted out her chin.

"It was my idea. Jeff could never have pulled it off without me. We all helped: Larry, Randy, Jeff, and me. I did most of the work, but this was a big sting, and I was supposed to get the biggest cut."

Monica couldn't believe what she had just heard. "But you just met Mrs. Harkenstone."

"That was the plan. I would never see her. But I changed my mind once I was here, and I added a little frill with the tee shirts and stuff," he bragged. "That was a spontaneous extra. The crazy, old lady didn't connect me with the Moonbeam Travel Agency. No one did!"

"You completely fooled me," moaned Monica.

"Me, too," added Leslie.

"Yeah, you fooled me, too. I knew you were a scheming bastard, but I had no idea you were part of the swindle," Sheila admitted while she glared at him. Her dogs yipped even louder when they sensed their mother was upset.

John had a pleased smile on his face. "I fooled everyone," he boasted. "It was my idea. Jeff would do most of the scam on the old lady because he was a nice looking, clean cut man. Randy, as secretary, would fake details about the trip and meet with her as needed. Larry had important contacts that got us the shell company, that phony Southwest Consulting Firm. But it was my idea. I worked it all out!"

Another voice was heard behind John. "John, I believed in you. I thought you were wonderful," wailed

Jessica who was wringing her hands while a few tears slid down her cheeks.

"Run, Jessica, go get help," screamed Monica. "Can't you see he has a gun!"

Jessica seemed unable to move as she stood there with her shoulders shaking. John moved back a few paces and waved the gun at her and then back to the other women. "God damn it! What are you doing here?"

"I followed your car. I thought you were seeing another girl," sobbed Jessica.

"Get in the room and stand with those others. I'm going to lock you all in, and by the time somebody lets you out, I'll be long gone. I'll be sipping martinis in Brazil," boasted John. He waved his gun back and forth in a shaky fashion as he indicated Jessica should move. She dragged her feet inside, stood by Monica, and bawled loudly. Forgetting the rule about not moving, Monica put her arms around Jessica.

"Look what you've done to this girl. She's lost her idealism. She'll never get it back, you big jerk," scolded Monica in her teacher voice.

"Give me the money! I've got to get going."

"How are you going to carry it? You can't put it in your pockets. You've got eight stacks of bills divided into packets with rubber bands around them. Each stack is about five inches high," said Sheila in a practical way.

"Put it in a bag!"

"There isn't a bag in the drawer. You didn't bring one with you, did you. Just like a man. You didn't think," reprimanded Sheila.

Flabbergasted, John let his eyes roam around the room for a bag. No bags, no suitcases, no boxes, just furniture. " Throw me a packet," he ordered.

Sheila lobbed one towards him. He picked it up and tried to stuff it in his pants pocket, but it fell out. He stuck it behind his belt. To accommodate the width, he had to unbuckle the belt. While fumbling around, the money fell again. He still held the gun, but it pointed in different directions as he ineffectively tried to stow away the packet of bills. All four women tittered behind their hands.

Sheila whispered, "In the movies, the woman detective rushes the guy with the gun. What about it, girls? There are four of us. We could knock him over, get the gun, and sit on him. Too bad no one has a tape recorder to get his confession about the fraud."

"Not me, I'm a chicken," said Leslie.

"We need a weapon," said Monica. "If we had a bat or a big board, it might work."

"Stop talking!" roared John who in his frustration had let the money slip out of his belt again. Now he balled up the packet of bills and stuck it down his open shirt. That worked.

"Throw me another packet," he ordered.

Sheila quickly grabbed another packet, removed the rubber band, and threw the money his way. The money scattered in all directions like leaves from a tree. John's mouth dropped open. Sheila seized another packet and did the same thing.

"God damn it, Sheila! Pick them up."

Monica also got into the spirit and tossed money at him. Money was floating everywhere. John had no idea what to do. His hair was mussed, and his shirt had sweat stains under the arms. He picked up a few bills around his feet while keeping the gun more or less aimed at the four women. Leslie and even Jessica with tears still rolling down her cheeks joined in the fun of flinging $100 bills in the air.

During all this time, the dogs kept barking non-stop. While John was bent over in an attempt to grab as many bills as he could, Leroy, holding one of his big signs that said "Kill the Evil Doers," appeared at the door. He lifted the wooden placard and banged it down on John's head with a heavy thump. As John crumpled, the gun fell out of his hand. Leroy kicked the gun which whizzed under the sofa.

Jessica ran over to him, threw her arms around his shoulders, and blubbered, "My hero!" Leroy dropped his sign and hugged Jessica.

The three women hugged each other and yelled, "Hurrah! Good for you, Leroy." In their joy, they tossed some money in the air, but this time it was a gesture of triumph. The dogs recognized the happy atmosphere and changed their barking to yips of joy.

"I was following you, Jessica. I wanted to talk to you. I saw you going into that unit, and I heard that dumb John yelling at you. So I went back to my car and got the only weapon I could find," explained Leroy while he had his arms around Jessica.

Into this party scene walked Rick with several uniformed cops. "What in the world?" he gasped as he took in the bizarre scene.

Everyone began to talk at once to Rick. After the entire story was told and retold, Monica put a literary spin on the episode. "Leroy saved the day. He defeated the evil doer with his evil doer sign. Isn't that wonderful poetic justice? I just love the way he nailed the criminal."

After singing out her delight, she continued, "John confessed he originated the entire sting operation and was going to take the money and run. He bragged about his cleverness. He said in a few hours he would be drinking martinis in a foreign country, but now he's out cold and in a few hours will be in jail. So this event gives us a literary example of irony."

The uniformed officers hand cuffed John and tucked him into the back of a police car. After all the tension, the women laughed with relief and hugged Leroy. Jessica grabbed his hand and said again, "My hero!"

The policemen scooped up the money and put all of it in a locked box that would stay in the evidence room at the police station until all the legalities were finished. Monica hoped the members of the Church of the Sun and Moon would be able to make their trip. She didn't know what percentage of the money was left, but there seemed a lot all over the floor of the storage unit.

After all the chaos was over, Sheila announced to the group, " I was going to rush over and kick John, you know where. But Leroy hit him before I had the chance."

Days later, Monica and Rick sat in her living room drinking red wine while discussing the events of "The Grand Finale at Number 68 at the Honest Abe Storage." Rick shook his head, "I've never had such a crazy end to a case. When I walked in, I saw $100 bills floating in the air, women yelling, dogs barking their heads off, and a man lying unconscious on the floor. I found out Leroy took out the crook with a sign that said 'Kill the Evil Doers' and now has become a hero to the fair maiden, Jessica. What an ending!"

"I have just one question. Who killed Jeff?" asked Monica. "I was surprised when I found out John was involved in the sting, but I still don't know who's the murderer."

"I think you know who it is by instinct. I have some facts which I'll tell you after you tell me who the killer is," bantered Rick as he took a sip of wine.

"John. My guess is John because he found out Jeff was skimming off the top. All those bank deposits were quite a bit lower than the checks Mrs. Harkenstone made out to the travel agency. What a blow to the ego. The super swindler ripped off by his own accomplice."

"Yes, you're right. John poisoned Jeff, and we have evidence to prove it. We found traces of the insecticide on his clothes. He even made a big mistake by leaving his fingerprints on the bottle of poisoned water. Remember the bottle cap had an X on it. He put it on after Jeff had drunk from it and died. I think he realized he could exploit the X and make it seem he was the intended victim which became a wonderful cover."

"What about the green van?"

"John rented it so that he could follow Sheila. He couldn't use his Prius since you or she would recognize it."

"He was clever, but not clever enough. Do you think Randy knew Jeff was skimming a lot of money off the top?" asked Monica.

"Yes, because she was around the office and probably saw the checks and the bank deposits. He must have made some arrangement with her to split this extra cash. However, he didn't tell her where he kept the money or she would have squirreled it away herself. She's taking a plea agreement with the District Attorney and will testify against John."

"What will happen to Larry?"

"He'll go on trial, unless he takes a plea. There's so much evidence against them that they'll all be doing time. John, probably, will spend his life in prison. Mrs. Harkenstone will get the money found in the storage shed back, but it wasn't all there. Who knows how much he spent on food, clothes, or whatever." Rick leaned back on the sofa and smiled at Monica. "A very satisfying end."

"Very satisfying, indeed. I hoped, however, Sheila could get some of the money. When I saw her yesterday, she was all packed up for her trip back home.

Strange thing, those dogs didn't have their little pink sweaters on, and they didn't look nearly as chubby. Could it be possible?"

"We'll never know," murmured Rick, "Are you going to write about this case and put it in a novel?

"No, I'm not. No one would ever believe it."

"Well, as the bard wrote, 'All's well that ends well,'" he said. She smiled when he quoted their favorite writer. With that encouragement, Rick placed his arm around her and gave her a very long, wonderful kiss.